DEADLY TEMPTATION

DEADLIEST LOVE
BOOK 1

HOLLY BLOOM

DARK BLOOM PUBLISHING

If you've ever wanted to stomp on an ex-boyfriend's balls with high heels, this one's for you.
You're better off without him.

PROLOGUE
IVY

THAT NIGHT...

His eyes burn like lasers, scorching into my arse as I head to the bar for my third drink. A smile stretches across my lips as I sway my hips dramatically. If he's looking, why not give him a show? After all, there's no better way to get over someone than getting under someone else.

Before I get a chance to order, the bartender slides another Pornstar Martini towards me—my favourite. I reach for my purse, but he stops me.

"This is on him," he says, nodding at the drop-dead gorgeous man sitting alone at a table a few feet away.

The same sexy stranger who has been checking me out all night. He tips his glass in my direction. Cute, but he'll have to do better than that if he wants to impress me.

I play it cool, sliding onto a high stool and soaking up the atmosphere. The bar is dripping in decadence from its chandeliers, fine art, and marble floors to a pianist playing in the background. This is where Spencer and I had our first date. It's only fitting that it's where I come to forget the six months I wasted on him. Fucker. He doesn't deserve more of my headspace. Leaving him is the best decision I've ever made, and this is my celebration.

"Here's to new beginnings," I whisper in a toast.

Another glass chimes against mine, making me jump and almost spill my precious drink over the sides.

A deep voice speaks in a low rumble, sending flutters straight up my thighs. "Cheers."

It's him.

I arch my eyebrow. "Thanks for the drink."

Up close, he's even better-looking. I'm talking Calvin Klein model with a chiselled jawline that'd rival Superman. His dark wavy hair sits around his shoulders, streaked with a few strands of grey. This isn't a random fuck-boy. He's a real man with a perfectly maintained beard who smells of a delicious aftershave that makes my knees weak.

I flick my hair over my shoulder and push my tits forward. His gaze travels down my body and lingers on my cleavage. Thank God I'm wearing my good bra!

"Are you waiting for someone?" he asks. His voice is smooth like butter but with a stormy edge, like rainfall followed by a lightning storm.

"No," I reply, turning my head to face him and batting my eyelashes. "I'm alone."

The Adonis wears an expensive black suit, like all the pretentious fuckers here. But unlike them, he pulls it off. He wears the suit, not the other way around. Jeans aren't part of the dress code in one of London's most exclusive bars. You need a membership to get past the bouncer, and I only got through the door because I name-dropped my jealous ex. Spencer Bexley has a reputation.

The corners of his mouth twitch, forming an easy half-smile. "In that case, you won't mind if I join you."

Usually, I'd tell a rando hitting on me where to go, but I don't. Instead, I sip my drink to showcase my dick-sucking abilities like a horny teenager. He takes the bait. His pupils dilate as he glances at my lips for a few seconds too long. *Jesus, Ive, what are you doing?* I stop myself from getting carried away and deep-throating the straw.

His eyes are unlike any I've seen before. They're sparkling amber jewels, but his left eye looks like a setting sun melting into a pool of dazzling blue.

"It's called heterochromia," he says, breaking the hypnotic trance. I splutter, spraying my drink. He acts quickly, offering me a napkin to dab away the mess dribbling down my chin. So much for acting cool. "My eyes. The colour. It's heterochromia."

"Oh, r-right," I stammer. "I knew that."

"I'm sure you did," he replies playfully.

He's oblivious to a nearby group of women gawping over his gorgeousness. Having his full attention makes my skin tingle, and I cross my legs, which is a struggle in a dress as tight as this one.

"What's your name?" I've not seen him around. He has a face you'd commit to memory for your next date with a vibrator. "I don't recognise you."

"I'm Freddie," he says. He picks up his glass, drawing attention to the prominent veins over his hands. My eyes roam higher. His crisp white shirt is rolled up to his elbows, showcasing muscled forearms. *Give me strength.* "I've been working overseas for a few years, but I'm home now. There's nowhere in the world like London."

What does he do for a living? He must be a millionaire to be a member here. He doesn't strike me as a banker—

those boring bastards are easy to spot because they use the state of the stock market to open a conversation. He's not a lawyer, either—they're uptight, always splashing their cash and boasting about how much things cost. I don't think he's someone who has inherited money. Trust fund brats love to party and have non-stop holidays, but I can't rule it out as a possibility. He looks to be in his mid-thirties, so his partying days could be behind him.

"And what's your name?" he asks.

"Daisy," I blurt out the first name that comes to mind.

My sister's name.

Spencer can't find out about his ex having a drink with another guy so soon after our breakup. He wouldn't take it well.

"You don't look like a Daisy," Freddie remarks. He has a posh British accent laced with something else. French? Swiss? I can't tell. Something European. "People say our names tell us a lot about who we are. A daisy is simple, understated, and delicate. Some would even say fragile. You don't strike me as any of those things."

"And you can tell all that just by looking at me?" I snort, calling bullshit. "What kind of name should I have then?"

He moves closer, engulfing me in his delicious smell and taking my breath away. Smokey, sweet, intoxicating. I press my thighs together. Holy hell, what kind of pheromones is he putting out? I'm acting like a hungry vampire waking from a century-long sleep. Maybe it's a build-up of sexual frustration from Spencer being a one-pump chump.

"Something royal," Freddie purrs, sweeping a rogue strand of hair off my face with his index finger. A bolt of desire races through my body at his touch. "You have the kind of face that steals a man's breath away and eyes that'll make him bow down at your feet and kill for you."

If he's offering to bow down before me, sign me the fuck up. I try to drag my mind out of the gutter, but I'm already under his spell.

"Are you offering to be my knight in shining armour?" I ask. "Because I don't need a man to save me."

"Beautiful and independent," he says appreciatively. "I like that. Why don't you tell me more about yourself?"

Guys who want to get into your pants usually skip the small talk, but Freddie doesn't seem to be in a rush to leave.

"About me?" I'm drawing a blank after becoming accustomed to Spencer talking for hours about himself. "I'm really not that interesting."

"I'm sure that's not true," he replies. "I want to know more about you. What do you do? Do you have a boyfriend? Any kids? What about your family?"

"I'm not here for an interrogation," I tease, then roll my eyes. "But if you must know, I'm between jobs right now. No boyfriend or kids... and my family... well, I have my sister." He listens intently. I should stop talking, but I keep going. "My parents died in a car accident, so it's just the two of us. We're really close, even though we're complete opposites. We've always been there for each other. She's got a cute puppy called Pippy, who is part of our family too... Anyway, enough about me! What's your story?"

"You're lucky to have your sister," he says wistfully, finishing his drink. "I don't have any family left. They were... there was... it's just me now."

My eyes widen. I want to learn more but don't want to ask and seem like an insensitive bitch.

"But I've thrown myself into work," he says, putting an

end to the subject. "I keep myself busy, and I came back to London for a change. Maybe it's time I meet someone special and settle down."

"Do you want kids?" I ask.

"Yes," he replies without hesitation. *Rest in peace, ovaries.* "One day."

I imagine cute ginger kids with impeccable jawlines running around a garden and playing games. What the hell is wrong with me?

I clear my throat as he leans forward. His body is inches from mine, a wall of pure muscle and warmth.

"Do you want to get out of here?" he whispers, his lips brushing against my earlobe. "I'm staying at the Royal Duchess. It'll be quieter there."

I know the place: the only hotel nearby, and the most expensive in London. The waiting list to get a room is months long. Fuck it. This is my celebration. The night I leave Spencer in the past. I snatch my handbag and slide off the stool. My skirt rides up my thighs to show him what he has to look forward to.

When Freddie takes my hand, a surge of electricity jolts my body as our fingers interlock. At six foot three, he dwarfs me, despite my ridiculous four-inch heels that are a broken ankle waiting to happen.

Under normal circumstances, I'm a three-date girl. But this is an exceptional case. A mysterious, handsome stranger is not someone I meet every day, especially in a part of the capital filled with zillionaires. I'm no gold digger. Money doesn't matter, but a guy who is kind *and* wealthy is like finding a golden unicorn with a rainbow tail.

"Enjoy your evening, Mr James," the host says, bowing

his head as we leave. His eyes narrow suspiciously in my direction. "Miss Penrose."

I ball my spare hand into a fist, resisting the urge to flip my middle finger. I won't be back. Freddie holds the door open for me, and we head onto the tree-lined Mayfair street. The buildings are gorgeous—beautiful grey brick with perfectly symmetrical windows. It's a far cry from the Hackney estate I lived in when I first moved to the capital, with overspilling bins, potholes in the road, and people stumbling out of kebab shops like the walking dead. We're in the same city, but it's a different world.

"Here." Freddie stops to take off his jacket and drape it around my shoulders. "You must be freezing."

"Thanks," I murmur gratefully. It drowns me, hanging down around my knees, but it's still toasty from his residual heat.

What is it about him that's making me break all my new rules? Chivalry is sweet and all, but I should have learned my lesson. The last man who wanted to take care of me turned out to be a controlling psychopath. But I remind myself, *I'm not Ivy tonight. I'm someone else.*

"I forgot how cold it gets," he comments.

The brisk winter breeze chills our cheeks, and I thank the stars I applied a generous layer of lip balm.

"Uh-huh," I say. "They say it might snow next week."

You're not British unless you make at least one comment about the weather in a conversation. For a small island, the changing climate provides ample opportunity for a country of socially awkward people to interact.

But Freddie's right. It *is* freezing. February has been bitterly cold—the kind of temperature that makes your ears throb. My red strapless dress wasn't a sensible choice, but it's the only dress Spencer didn't attack with scissors in a fit of rage when I told him we were over.

"We won't have far to go until we're back in the warmth," he reassures. "It's just up ahead."

I catch our reflections in a closed shop window. I've lost weight over the past few months, but I'm still a curvy girl, and I feel tiny next to Freddie. His jacket makes me look like I've shrunk in the wash. My strawberry-blonde hair bounces around my shoulders in loose waves as we walk. I imagine we're characters in a film, then… *Fuck.*

My outrageous heel slips between a crack in the pavement, holding my ankle hostage as firm hands around my waist stop me from falling over.

"Nice reflexes," I remark, grateful my red cheeks can be explained by the wind and not his steady grip.

I've read about strangers having an instant spark and dismissed it as fiction, but that's how I feel now. We've just met, but it's as if we've known each other for years. Being in his company is easy. It's hard to describe, but something about him makes me feel safe. Like he can be trusted.

Freddie's eyes meet mine, and he says, "I'll always catch you."

And I believe him. We stand frozen on the empty street, locked in a stare neither of us wants to break. An overhead streetlamp shrouds us in an orange glow as I tip my chin up to meet the light.

He strokes my cheek, and his rough calluses startle me. Rich men usually have smooth hands from not working a day in their life, but Freddie's touch tells another story. He's worked hard. Really fucking hard. A shudder of desire ignites in my core. How else is this man going to take me by surprise?

Our world slows, and a black cab crawls past. I pay no

attention to the vehicle as Freddie's muscular arm slides under his jacket, resting on the small of my back. Then he bends to kiss me.

My heart rate quickens, pumping at triple speed as our lips meet. We get swept away in a fairy tale. His lips are soft and full, gentle to start but packed with underlying longing and a fiery urge for *more*.

I grab his shirt, yanking him closer.

His hands run through my hair as I push my body against his, pressing my tits into his chest. His cock hardens, leaving me under no illusion that he wants me as much as I want him… and that he's going to be as big as he looks.

It's a kiss that makes my stomach flutter with an army of butterflies. It's a kiss that would wake a princess from a long snooze. It's a kiss that I know, for whatever subconscious reason, will become a defining moment in my life. After this, nothing will be the same again…

I sense his feelings from how our tongues dance and how emotion layers his kiss—sadness, anguish, happiness, an outpouring of whatever makes him the person he is. It's packed with a desperate yearning and a primal instinct. A sense that this is meant to be. That *we* are meant to be.

He catches my bottom lip between his teeth, drawing an unstoppable moan from me. This is an affluent neighbourhood and not a street where you kiss in public—especially the type of kiss that makes you want to tear each other's clothes off. But having to wait another few minutes to return to the hotel isn't enough. His cock twitches, begging to be let free.

"Fuck." Freddie pulls away breathlessly for a second, looking down at me in awe. "You're unlike any other woman I've met."

Before I can reply, he kisses me again. His giant hands slide over my round arse and squeeze hard, while I trace my fingers over his muscles through his shirt. He's rocking hard abs and a six-pack that would put underwear models to shame.

"I want you," I whisper into his mouth between kisses.

"I don't want you," he growls. "I *need* you."

A blue Ford Focus slows beside us, beeping incessantly. I'd recognise that old shit heap anywhere, even if my sister's disapproving voice wasn't shouting from the rolled-down window.

"Hey, over here!" Daisy is two years younger than me, but she's always been the sensible one. I shield my eyes before the bright headlights almost blind me. "Is that you?"

"Shit," I mutter. "I forgot my sister was picking me up. I didn't think she'd be here this early."

Her beeping grows more frantic as she pounds the horn incessantly and yells, "Get in!"

Can't she see I'm in the middle of something? Daisy doesn't go out often, preferring to curl up on the sofa and binge romance books. For someone who enjoys reading monster smut, she's being incredibly inconsiderate of my current situation.

"I'm sorry, but I'm going to have to go," I say reluctantly, knowing she'll pull an unbearable hissy fit if I tell her to leave without me. "I'm leaving London for a few weeks and heading back to our family home. I've got nowhere else to go while I'm in between places. She's my ride."

He smirks. "You can stay with me."

"Nice try," I say, although I don't think he's joking. "You better take your jacket—"

"No, keep it," he insists, stopping me from taking it off like a true gentleman. A smoking hot gentleman whose bones I want to jump. "You can return it to me when we see each other again."

"So, you want to see me again?" The Focus comes to a halt alongside us and honks. I turn to scream at Daisy's glowering face. "Give me one fucking minute!" Then I face Freddie again, softening my voice. "I really am sorry…"

"I don't make a habit of inviting a beautiful woman to my hotel room," Freddie says. Why, oh why, did I not tell Daisy to leave without me earlier? "I want to get to know you." He drops his voice, and his breath tickles my neck as he leans in to whisper, "In every way."

My clit swells. Yep, she's going to be decimated by my new vibrator later. Hopefully, Daisy has spare batteries.

"She'll lose her shit if I don't get into the car in the next thirty seconds," I mumble, hoping my words are coherent. "Thanks for the drink. It was… great… to meet you."

"My number's in the jacket pocket," Freddie says. "Call me when you get back."

"It might be a few hours. Our cottage is on the coast," I say. "You'll probably be asleep."

"I won't be until I know you've arrived safely." He smiles, making the fine lines wrinkle around his sparkling eyes. "Call me."

I nod. My legs are shaky without his arms around me, and I totter to the car like a toddler learning to walk.

"I'll see you soon, Daisy," he promises.

My sister's head whips around. I shoot her a *don't say a fucking word unless you want to be disowned* glare. She huffs, taking the hint, and taps her fingers impatiently on the wheel.

"Uh-huh, you will," I reply. Seeing my red lipstick

smudged on his collar fills me with satisfaction. "Goodbye, Freddie."

———

Years later, I keep coming back to the same question…

How could an evening that started so perfectly turn into the worst night of my life?

CHAPTER 1
IVY

My freshly dyed fiery hair trails to my waist in loose curls. Red's my favourite colour, like the pools of blood I leave my targets in.

It's been a few months since I returned to England at Alaric's special request. I'd rather have stayed in Europe, travelling around Italy, France, and Spain. I was never in the same place long—just how I liked it. But it's been five years, and my boss needs me. I owe Alaric my life. Helping him is the least I can do.

Being back in London is strange. The city used to be my home, but walking through the familiar streets puts me on edge. You can never be too careful in my line of work, so I'm always looking over my shoulder.

I sip my champagne and pretend to listen as the man on stage continues his speech. An up-and-coming tech company is throwing a huge office party to celebrate its IPO, and around two hundred people are here. They don't have a typical office, though. It's more like a resort. It has an entertainment suite, gym, pool, and bottomless break-fast bar—everything to ensure you never leave.

The crowd laughs at the male speaker's corny joke. Adam Brentwood is the company co-founder. He's not my mark, but the man beside him is. Danny Oliver, the other co-founder, is the real brain behind the operation and the man who needs to die. The man I'm going to kill.

I don't ask questions. That's not my job. When people pay for our services, we deliver. Our promise of discretion makes the Killers Club the best group of assassins to hire.

Across the room, Stephanie—my partner for the evening—flirts with a group of neckbeards who are delusional enough to believe she's interested in them. Newsflash: *She's not.* If something seems too good to be true, it usually is. Unfortunate genetics aside, why would anyone be attracted to men who haven't showered for weeks?

Stephanie catches my eye and smirks. She's a blonde bombshell who turns heads wherever she goes. She's as good at playing decoy as she is at cleaning up crime scenes, and the group is eating out of the palm of her hand.

I check my watch. The speech should finish soon. Drinks will be served, and Danny will return to his office. He never stays at a party for long, or so our source tells us.

My fingers buzz with the familiar excited anticipation before a kill. Killing isn't just a job, it's my purpose. Something I'm wholly desensitised to. That, and my thirst for revenge, is what I live for. Although revenge takes time, so I have to be patient. Waiting will only make it sweeter.

The speech ends. Out of the corner of my eye, I see Stephanie nod—a tiny motion only I detect. I circle the room and blend in with the others. My black dress is an acceptable level of slutty for the occasion. It's cut low enough to tease my cleavage but sits above the knees to keep it business casual.

The co-founders leave the stage to claps and cheers from an admiring audience while tasteful violin music plays to give an air of sophistication. Workers, investors, journalists, and industry experts are all in attendance. The company must make a good impression ahead of its next funding round.

The workers, in particular, are taking full advantage of the free bar. Who can blame them when they spend the rest of the year stuck behind a screen bashing out code?

I watch Adam and Danny from a distance. Adam has a lot to gain from Danny's death. At first glance, he doesn't look like the type who wants his partner dead. They seem to get on well, smiling and joking together. I can't know for sure that Adam is our client. Alaric is the only one who knows their identities, but most of the time, I can figure it out.

There. Adam's eyes narrow as he shoots Danny a side glare. *That look.* Adam's trying to hide it, but I see the festering resentment, jealousy, and hungry greed that says he'll do anything to get what he wants. When you know what to look for, it's easy to spot.

The men part ways. Adam is smart to surround himself with a group of eyelash-fluttering airheads. They'll be a fantastic alibi when he inevitably falls under suspicion— not that Danny's death will look like a murder when I'm finished.

"The cameras are disabled," Penelope says through an earpiece. It's hidden behind my hair and small enough that no one will detect it. Penelope is our tech wizard and can hack into any system in the world. She's also a recluse who rarely leaves her office. I've only seen her once in five years, and only because Stephanie dragged her out.

It's go-time.

I follow Danny through the windowless corridors. The carpet muffles my footsteps as I lurk in the shadows. He takes a right turn, then a left, right, straight, and left again. I press my back against the wall as he clicks his office door closed behind him.

A few minutes pass. He can't think he's been followed. *Prepare for action.* I reapply my lipstick and fluff up my hair before turning the handle and stumbling inside.

"Sorry," I say in a fake American accent. "I got a little lost. I'm looking for the restroom?"

"It's at the end of the corridor." Danny looks up from behind his thick glasses and scowls. "Didn't you see the signs?"

"I must have missed them," I say, twirling a curl around my finger. "Oh my gosh. You're Danny Oliver, aren't you?"

His lips press into a disapproving line. "Yes."

"I've heard so much about you," I babble, edging closer to his desk. His beady eyes stray to my chest. "I've seen you in the news. I know this sounds silly…" I put my hand up to my mouth, making sure I squeeze the twins together. "But I'd love an autograph."

He snaps out of my tit trance. "I don't do autographs."

"But I've brought a magazine," I say, placing my bag on his desk and rummaging around inside it.

As I pull out the magazine, I clumsily knock the bag over. A purse, umbrella, and various other objects—including a bottle of pills—roll across the wooden floor. I drop to my knees to pick up the mess.

"Speak to Adam," Danny grumbles. The fucker doesn't even move to help me. "He'll sign it."

For someone soon to be one of the wealthiest men in the country, you'd think he'd be in a better mood.

"It would be great to get your signature, too," I lie as I stand again. "You're both on the cover."

I hold out the carefully selected magazine and a pen. It looks like an ordinary pen but doubles as a syringe. I've plunged it into many marks to incapacitate them, but I'm not doing that to Danny. I want his death to be slow and subtle.

He sighs, realising I won't give up. "Fine."

He snatches them and scrawls over the cover, giving me a good view of the jumping pulse in his neck. A pulse that will stop soon.

Danny takes Adderall, a stimulant more common in the States, that increases concentration. Rumour has it, he has an addiction and can't function without them. He tenses as he leans back in his seat, noticing the label on the pills that have conveniently landed near his feet that I've failed to pick up.

"Thanks, Danny," I chirp as he thrusts the signed copy at me.

"It's no problem." His tone is more pleasant now that he thinks he's getting a free fix. "I hope you enjoy the rest of the party."

"I'm sure I will," I reply, folding up the magazine and stashing it in my bag. "Thanks again."

Another job to tick off my list.

The pills are laced with lethal amounts of thallium. By the time the effects kick in days later, I'll be long gone, and it'll be too late to save him. It's not my weapon of choice, but the method isn't up to me. Our clients get to choose how a target dies. It's all part of our Killers Club service.

"Job done?" Penelope asks in my ear.

"Confirmed," I whisper. "But I'm going to stick around for a while."

"Use the code word if you need to alert me," Penelope says, "but I'm signing off now."

I return to the party, now in full swing, while Stephanie's making her excuses to leave. She heads to the exit, much to her admirer's disappointment. She doesn't like hanging around after a job, but I'm not ready to go yet. Danny won't keel over his desk at any second, and my stomach's rumbling. Who can say no to a buffet? I head over, grab a paper plate and start loading it with as much food as it can hold when…

Fuck.

My heart skips a beat.

I see a face I recognise through the crowd. Slick black hair, broad shoulders, and a memorable thick wedding band on his finger engraved with a family crest. *Anthony Steel.* He was there that night. The night that changed my life five years ago. The night they killed my sister and left me for dead.

I abandon my plate and start pushing my way through the foyer. I haven't got a plan. I don't need one. All I have to do is get him alone for long enough to…

"Sorry." A clumsy idiot bumps into my shoulder and almost knocks me over. "I didn't look where I was going."

"Maybe you should get glasses," I snap back.

The stranger's shoulders block my view.

"Why don't you let me make it up to you?" the clutz suggests.

He moves slightly, and I can't see Anthony. *Fuck.* I can't lose him.

I look up at the man who has temporarily halted my plans. He pushes his blonde hair out of his face, and it falls in an effortlessly wind-swept way. He has the most piercing green eyes I've ever seen. Those, and his sharp cheekbones, could hypnotise someone into buying anything. He has a swimmer's build, but I'd bet he's stronger than he looks from the way his clothes fit his defined muscles. Underneath his white shirt, outlines of tattoos covering his chest are visible when the light hits him at a certain angle. He's hiding a wild side under his tux.

"I'm Seb." He holds out his hand with a cheeky smile. A smile that could melt a million girls' hearts yet puts my guard up instantly.

"Rose," I reply through gritted teeth, easily slipping into my fake identity. "I'm just leaving."

"Wait." He catches my wrist as I step past him. He's lucky I don't break his hand. "Why don't I buy you a drink to apologise?"

"It's a free bar."

"Fine, you've caught me," he says. "Maybe I've been looking for an excuse to talk to you."

"Really?" I plant my hands on my hips. "Does that line usually work?"

"Actually, yes," he replies with a mischievous grin. "But I mean it. I'd definitely sleep better knowing you're not concussed. Just stay another ten minutes, so I can be sure you're okay."

"I walked into you, not a wall," I reply. "But fine, I'll have one drink."

His face lights up. He's not a quitter, and until I see

Anthony again, it won't hurt to have an excuse to stick around.

I follow Seb to the bar. The crowd parts for him to pass, and we go straight to the front. British people don't break queuing rules unless there's someone important around. Who is this man? Should I know him?

"Champagne?" Seb offers. "Or wine?"

"Champagne," I say, hardly paying attention to him as I scan the sea of faces.

Goddammit. I spot Anthony, surrounded by three others, leaving the building. Even if I want to get to him, I can't. There are too many witnesses, and I want to take my time with him. Just like he did with Daisy.

Seb hands me a flute. Hushed whispers follow us as he leads me to a quiet booth, away from prying eyes.

"Do you work here?" he asks.

"No," I reply, pulling my fake press badge from my bag. "I'm writing a story about the IPO. I'm assuming, as you asked me, that you don't work here either?"

"No." He chuckles. "But I'm an investor."

Of course he is. He fits the bill for a rich, smart arse who likes to throw money around.

"But don't hold it against me," he says, reading my mind. "I'm not like the other investors you might have met."

I cross my arms. "Who says I'd hold it against you?"

"Your face," he says. "That, and how your eyebrows dipped when I said the word *investor*."

I sit up straighter. Not bad for an amateur. There's more to him than meets the eye, and now I'm intrigued.

"Do you make a habit of reading a stranger's body language?" I rebut, cocking my head to the side to study him. "Most people don't like being psychoanalysed. It's a conversation killer."

"You're a journalist," he replies. "Isn't reading body language something you do all the time?"

"I ask questions, too," I say. "Why are you still here, anyway? The other investors left after the speech."

"Perceptive, aren't you?" Seb drapes his arms over the back of the booth. "Maybe I fancied a night out. Staying worked in my favour, didn't it? Now I'm having a drink with the prettiest woman in the room."

His compliment floors me, and I avoid looking into his dreamy eyes.

"Are investors allowed to flirt with party guests?" I ask. "Do you want me to write a good story? Put your spin on it? What's your end game?"

Seb laughs. From his confidence, I'd guess he's in his early thirties but looks younger and gives me Leo DiCaprio in *Titanic* vibes. "Are you always so suspicious of people?"

I narrow my eyes. "That's my job."

His phone beeps. He checks it and swears under his breath.

"What's wrong?" I tease, unable to resist. "Is it past your bedtime?"

Seb takes his business card out of his pocket and slides it across the table. His shirt rides up his wrists to expose a tattoo wrapping around it. Does he have a full sleeve? "How would you like to finish our conversation over dinner next week?"

"Are you always this direct?" I challenge him. "We've just met."

"It's not every day I meet someone like you." His words send a shiver of longing down my spine. I've not felt like this in a long time, and the sensation is alien. "I want to know more about you, Rose…"

"Rose Hathaway," I finish his sentence. "And you are…" I pick up his card. "Sebastian Montgomery."

Why does that sound familiar? I'm missing something, and I'll kick myself when I remember.

"Just Seb," he says.

"Okay, just Seb," I say, turning the card over in my fingers. "I'll think about it."

"Good," he replies, "because I'd like to see you again."

I sip my champagne as he leaves. He gets into a waiting black car with bulletproof windows.

Who are you, Sebastian Montgomery?

CHAPTER 2
SEB

She's perfect, and I can't stop thinking about her. A natural beauty with perfect tits, teeth, and curves packed into a tight body she's worked hard for. Then, her snarky mouth… Fuck, that makes her even hotter.

No one talks to or challenges me like that, and I fucking love it. I've already had multiple cold showers thinking about what I'd do to her if I got her alone.

"Are you still sulking over me cutting your date short?" Freddie asks, raising his eyebrows. Callen snickers, while a sly grin spreads over Bram's face. Bastards. The lot of them.

"You can all fuck off," I say. "We have work to do."

"When you're not busy pining over a girl you met for two minutes," Callen teases. "Hasn't she called yet? How long has it been? A week?"

Eight days, to be exact, but who's counting?

"When are you going back to Edinburgh?" I glare at him. "You were supposed to be staying for a weekend, but it's been a year."

"What can I say? I'm starting to feel at home," Callen says, propping his feet up on our coffee table like he owns the fucking place. "I like it here."

"You know this is my house, don't you?" I snarl, wanting to wipe the smug look off his face. He's infuriating. "I can kick you out whenever I want."

My home became our base of business operations four years ago. Although we have a private agreement that the house is mine, the deeds are in Freddie's name. We transferred them after deciding someone might try to track a member of the royal family. On paper, I live in an empty flat on the other side of the city.

"But you won't," Freddie says coldly in his zero-bullshit tone. He's our boss, and what he says goes. "Because this is the Dukes' house now."

"See?" Callen taunts. "There's nothing you can do."

I clench my teeth to hold myself back. At first, we used the house solely as our place of work, but everyone stayed so often that it made sense for them to move in permanently. I can't say I'm happy about our most recent addition, however. Callen may be a Duke, but that doesn't mean I have to like him.

"We have a problem," Freddie says, cutting off our argument with a few taps on his keyboard. The projector screen rolls down from the ceiling. A big perk of being rich is having the coolest gadgets. This one is courtesy of the poor fucker who has just shown up dead. "Danny's death wasn't an accident. We failed, and now we have to find out who killed him." His expression hardens. "No one crosses the Dukes."

As well as not hearing from Rose, Danny's death is another source of my bad mood. Danny contacted us a month ago because he feared something like this would happen. His company was growing at an alarming rate. In five years, it's predicted to be one of the biggest companies in the world. I never liked the miserable twat, but I hate that someone killed him on our watch.

Freddie, Callen, Bram, and I are the Dukes. People, like Danny, hire us for protection. We're better than any security firm or gang. For the right price, we are the only people who can keep someone safe. We have resources, money, power, and discretion, but best of all? We have no fucking rules. If someone is coming for you, we'll kill them first. The Dukes will do whatever it takes to protect their customers, and we've had a flawless record… until now.

Callen flicks through our copy of the coroner's report in front of him. Once upon a time, he used to be a surgeon —hence the ego—but now puts his skills to other uses.

"His cause of death is listed as kidney failure, but I don't buy it. He was healthy with no previous problems," Callen summarises, shaking his head. "Judging by his symptoms, my bets are on a poison. There's no toxicology report, so I can't prove it, but I'd guess thallium. It's an unusual but effective choice. It's often misdiagnosed before it's too late. Thallium is slow-acting, just like Seb's new girl." He smirks, then continues, "It takes days to kick in. This wasn't an amateur job."

I swallow. "When do you think it happened?"

"Hard to say." Callen scrunches his nose to read handwriting that only a medical professional could decipher. "It depends on the dosage, but the only time he left his house was to go to the launch party. I think he crossed paths with his killer that night."

This is my fault. My ten-minute chat with Rose could have been all it took for the killer to slip past me. There were plenty of people in the room who would benefit from his death. We have to narrow down the suspect list.

I turn to Bram. "Where are we on CCTV?"

Bram shakes his head. He doesn't speak. He can't. Someone cut out half of his tongue before we met. He can sign and use text-to-speech on a special device Freddie bought him to communicate, but he rarely chooses to. I've grown to understand Bram from his head tilts and expressions. For someone who can't talk, he can be a real pain in my arse.

I don't know the details about Bram's history, but he's known Freddie for years. If Freddie trusts him, that's enough for me. Without trust, we have nothing.

"No CCTV," Freddie confirms. "Someone hacked into the feed and played it on loop. The security team, who were supposed to be watching, were too drunk to notice anything unusual."

"So, someone slipped into the party, gave Danny some kind of poison, and then it took days for him to die?" I scratch my chin. I don't know whether I'm more annoyed or impressed. "They're good."

"But we're better," Freddie says, smashing his fist down on the table. "We need to find out who did this before they compromise any more of our operations." He rises from his seat. His calm exterior hides his blazing fury. He cares about maintaining the Dukes' reputation more than anything. "I'm going out for dinner with a potential client. Callen, you're joining me."

Usually, I'm Freddie's number two. This is his way of punishing me, but it's not harsh enough. No matter how fucking perfect Rose Hathaway's curves are, I screwed up a job. The Dukes don't make mistakes.

CHAPTER 3
IVY

I drop-kick the punching bag and send it flying across the gym.

"Nice," Stephanie remarks, then winks. "You should text him."

I take a swig of water, still dripping with sweat from our combat training.

"I don't date," I reply.

My life is complicated enough with juggling killing sprees. I don't need to add a guy into the mix. Why invite extra drama into my life?

"You're going to be in London for a while," Stephanie says. "Being part of the club doesn't mean you can't enjoy your downtime. You need more balance. You're all work and no play."

Stephanie is the only person I know who can kill someone with zero remorse and still insist on meditating to cleanse your aura. Talk about a juxtaposition.

"This better not be another excuse to lecture me about Yoni eggs," I say, landing another punch on the bag with a satisfying thwack. "I'm not interested."

"Seeing him again will be good for you," she insists. "You said he was hot, right?"

Yeah, damn fucking hot. Like I'd eat off his body like a plate fucking hot.

"He's okay," I lie, thinking about Seb's gorgeous green eyes and the ink behind his clothes.

"I guess that means you're not interested in a background check on him, then…"

"What?" I freeze, suspending my fist in mid-air. "You ran a check on him?"

"I was curious," she says. "He's the first guy you've mentioned to me since I've known you who isn't a mark or on your hit list."

Stephanie and Alaric know about my list. When Alaric judges that the time is right, he'll let me work through it. Waiting for five years has tested my patience, but I've not faltered. I swore my loyalty to the Killers Club, and I've honoured that vow because I know the wait will be worth it.

"What did the check say?"

"I thought you didn't want to see him again…" Stephanie smirks. She has me, and she knows it. "You don't date, remember?"

She heads across the vast gym to her bag. We're in the training area of one of the club's many global bases. Our London headquarters is our most prominent and where she and Alaric spend most of their time. This is where I learned everything there is about killing and discovered my inner strength. It's the closest place to a home I'll get.

"I'm still not going to break my no-dating rule," I say, "but you may as well show me now that you've gone through all the trouble."

She fans a folder in front of her face. "So, you *do* want to find out more about him?"

Since we met, I've managed to resist running an internet search on Seb. If I don't plan on seeing him again, what would be the point? But the urge to find out more about him is too strong when she's laying it out on a plate.

"Give it to me," I growl, ready to charge at her.

"I will," she says. "On one condition."

"What is it?"

"You text him," she says, "and go on one date."

I call her bluff. "There can't be anything bad in his file if you want me to go out with him."

"Trust me, it's a juicy read." Stephanie waggles her eyebrows. "You're not going to want to pass this up."

"Okay, I'll go, but it's not a real date." I sigh in exasperation, swiping the folder from her fingers. "I'm only going because you blackmailed me."

She peers over my shoulder as I scan the page, my heart rate quickening at seeing his picture. How is it fair that some people hit the genetic lottery jackpot?

"He's hot," Stephanie admires.

"Holy shit." My eyeballs almost pop out of their sockets. I read it again to make sure I've not made a mistake. "He's basically a fucking prince?"

Now I understand why the crowds parted like Moses was in their midst at the party.

"Technically, he's twentieth in line to the throne," Stephanie says. "Even though he has blue blood, he seems to keep his distance from the royal family. Think of him as a Bruce Wayne-type figure. His family is loaded, and he invests money in tech companies. He avoids the public eye unless he has to. Apparently, he hasn't dated in years. I can't find a hint of him ever having a serious relationship anywhere."

"Isn't having no relationship history a giant red flag? Besides, he's too high profile," I say. "Or have you forgotten that being part of the club means trying to avoid attention? We're ghosts for a reason."

"Puh-lease." She rolls her eyes. "When else will you get a chance like this? Don't you want to find out more about him?" She points at his photograph. "Look at those cheekbones and dimples. If you don't call him, maybe I will."

She and Alaric have been an item for years, but that doesn't stop her from dating other men for information. She's the perfect honey trap. Alaric understands work comes first, but he's giving her fewer of those jobs now that we have more agents. He won't admit it, but he doesn't want to share her.

"No!" I object. Damn, I've shown her my hand. "I'll go, okay? I'll see him one more time, but that's it."

"Text him now," she says. "I need proof."

I try to wriggle out of it. "But I don't have his number on me."

"Are you telling me you didn't save it in your phone already?"

"I…" Okay, I saved his number, but only because you never know when it might come in handy. Stephanie sees straight through my act. "Fine, I'll do it now."

I grab my phone and draft the text. What should I say? I'm experienced in seducing men to kill them, although I haven't dated for years. I don't know what I'm doing.

So… when are we having the dinner you promised?

That'll do, won't it? Maybe he'll think I'm rude and demanding, so he won't reply at all. That'd be better for everyone.

"Perfect," Stephanie says as I hit send. "Playing hard to get."

"I'm not playing anything," I grumble. "I'm only doing this for you."

She winks. "Yeah, keep telling yourself that."

Alaric strides into the gym, and Stephanie's face falls as she reads his expression. It's creepy how in sync the two of them are.

"What's wrong, hun?" she asks.

Alaric's nostrils flare, and his tattooed hands ball into angry fists. Most people find Alaric intimidating. A forty-something monster with a shaven head and ridiculous muscles that can fill a doorframe, but he's like family to me. He's ruthless but fair and, right now, he's fucking pissed.

"It's Adam Brentwood," he growls.

"The client who ordered the hit on Danny?" I ask. Well, the guy I assumed did. Alaric never confirmed my suspicions. "What about him?"

The job went smoothly. Danny died, and no one suspects a thing. The coroner is on our payroll, so there was no toxicology report, and kidney failure was listed as his cause of death. It's the perfect crime, all neat and wrapped up in a pretty bow. Case closed.

"Adam has been taken," Alaric says.

"Taken?" Stephanie frowns. "Like, kidnapped?"

After we complete a job, he keeps in touch with our clients for a while. They pay good money, so we like to ensure they're happy. This is the first time someone has kidnapped a client so close to a kill. It can't be a coincidence.

"Yes, kidnapped," he snaps impatiently. "And there's more."

He holds up his phone to show us a photograph. He's gripping it so tightly that it's a miracle it hasn't been crushed. A picture sent from Adam is on the screen. I squint to see a scrawled note that says:

Now we're even.
The Dukes.

"The Dukes?" I rack my brain to see if I remember a gang with that name, but nothing. "Who are they?"

"Penelope's working on it now," Alaric says. "She's digging up everything she can find on them."

"Who do you think the message is for?" I ask, although I already know the answer.

"Us," Alaric confirms. His jaw is set in a firm line. Skulls are going to get smashed. "The Dukes, whoever they are, are drawing battle lines. If they want a battle, we'll bring them a fucking war."

The Dukes have picked the wrong people to mess with. They'd better watch out.

CHAPTER 4

SEB

"This might hurt a little," Callen says. His terrifying maniacal grin gives a glimpse of his inner psychopath.

Adam bawls like a baby as Callen grips his tooth with the pliers. I yawn, standing with my back against the cold brick wall of our hidden basement room, and watch from the shadows.

"What's wrong?" Callen taunts. He loves toying with them. "Don't you like the dentist?"

The Dukes are protectors, but this is a special case. This time, we're protecting ourselves and our stellar reputation.

I don't wince as Callen tears the tooth from Adam's gums, spraying blood everywhere like a Jackson Pollock painting. The metal tray clinks as he drops the canine next to the others, lining them up in a neat row.

"Don't make it any more difficult than it needs to be," Freddie says. He perches on a stool nearby, watching with indifference as Adam gurgles on his blood. "All you have to do is tell us what happened to Danny."

Since his arrival, the bastard has been lying through his

teeth, hence their removal. Adam profited the most from Danny's death and judging by how he pissed himself when we showed up, he's hiding something. My instincts are rarely wrong. Adam is the slippery snake responsible for Danny's death, but he lacks the spine to get his own hands dirty. All we're interested in is who he hired to do it.

Callen returns to the workbench. It's stocked with tools, saws, chisels, and various pieces of surgical equipment—essentially a torturer's wet dream. We're in the business of protection, so extracting information is par for the course… and we do it well. When the Dukes are done, people spill their darkest secrets. It's a shame none of them ever leave the room, but that's why we're good at what we do. We never leave a trace behind.

My anger rises as I check my watch. It's been three hours, and my patience is waning.

"Tell us what you know, Adam," I say. "Crying or praying won't help you. No one can hear you down here."

Iceberg builds are the newest trend in London. There's no space to expand above ground, so the rich are constructing vast underground lairs. Most want a swimming pool, spa, or tennis court, but we're more creative.

"I don't…" Adam's voice trails off as he sobs, making blood spout from his mouth like a water fountain.

I roll up my sleeves and turn to Callen. "Let me try." The next part is going to get messy. I can persuade Adam to comply. "Bram, why don't you help me out?"

It's easy to forget Bram is around. He observes the unfolding scene like a statue, but he springs into action. He picks up a power drill and plugs it into the wall.

A twisted grin spreads over my face. "Perfect."

"Please," Adam begs, flailing around. There's nowhere to go. He's strapped down, his ankles and wrists tied. The chains holding him are strong enough to restrain a grizzly. "I don't know what you're talking about."

Wrong answer. My annoyance amplifies. Apart from interrogating him, we brought him here to make a statement and warn Danny's killer. If they fuck with us again, we'll come for them next.

"Knowing nothing is pretty convenient when your business partner was poisoned, and you're set to take over the entire company," I say, ignoring Adam's pathetic objections. "Did you know Danny was in the process of changing his will? He wanted to protect his assets and make sure his company shares were protected."

"No one said he was poisoned. He died of kidney failure," Adam says. "We've known each other since we were kids. I'd never hurt him."

His lies reek more than his urine soaking through his trousers.

"Cut the crap," I yell. I turn on the drill, and its whirr echoes around the basement like a death knell. Thankfully, the walls are sound-proofed. "Callen, get the pliers too."

"No, no, no," Adam objects as Callen rips off his shoes and socks. "Oh God, no!"

Callen doesn't wait for further instructions. He rips Adam's big toenail off, making him squeal like a pig.

I step closer and bend down, hovering the drill over his temple.

"If you were Danny's friend, I'd hate to see how you treat your enemies," I hiss.

"We know you ordered the kill," Freddie steps in, making me step back. "All you have to do is tell us who you paid to do it. We know you didn't pull it off yourself. You're good at talking to the cameras, but you're not a killer." Adam doesn't answer, so Freddie sighs. "Over to you, Seb."

Snot drips down Adam's swollen face. The fear in his eyes fuels me. He may not have force-fed Danny poison, but he's the reason our client died.

I turn on the drill again, making Adam thrash around more. He struggles against the binds he'll never be free from.

"You don't have long to start talking," I purr, holding the drill to his ear. The sound will rattle his brain and make his bones shake.

I get closer and closer. The tip of the drill grazes his skin, and that's all it takes for him to say, "Okay, okay, I'll tell you… Just don't hurt me, okay? If I tell you, you have to let me go."

I pause.

"We don't want to hurt you, Adam," Freddie lies, lulling the rat into a false sense of security. "Tell us what we want to know, then we'll let you go."

Adam relaxes a little, reassured by the man in a nice suit. Freddie plays the good cop, but he's worse than the rest of us. He presents as a charming gentleman, but he's a vicious wolf underneath. He spent years in law enforcement following the rules, but he knows true justice only happens when you take it into your own hands.

"Someone told me about a club," Adam says. "When I asked around, I found out more. You pay to become a member. Then they'll kill whoever you want in whatever way you want."

"What do this club call themselves?" Callen asks.

"The Killers Club."

"How fucking original," I mutter sarcastically.

Bram tenses. He's paying attention now. He'll be

thinking the same thing I am. How long have a group of assassins lived under our noses? This is the Dukes' territory. How many more deaths are they responsible for, and how long will it be until they kill another one of our clients? They have to be stopped.

"How did you find them?" Freddie asks sharply. He's trying not to show it, but Adam has piqued his interest.

"I went to a few clubs, then someone slipped me a card one night," he says. "I don't know the guy. I never spoke to him again."

"What did he look like?" Freddie questions.

"He's tall," Adam says.

I switch on the drill. "We need you to be a little more descriptive than that."

"Okay, okay! Just turn that off, please?" Adam squeezes his eyes shut in concentration. "Brown hair, around six foot tall, in his late twenties. He's built. Really fucking built. He must spend hours in the gym every week."

"You're describing half of London," I say.

"He has a scar," Adam says. "A raised scar on his neck. It's diagonal, going from the left to the right. It looks like his throat has been cut."

"Was the man who gave you the card the same person you spoke to when you called the number?" Freddie probes.

"I'm not sure," Adam says. "All I did was pay their membership fee, and then he asked questions and told me about their different packages."

"Packages?" Callen scowls. "What kind of packages?"

The Killers Club has turned death into an exclusive members-only business. Genius, but twisted.

"It depends on who you want to kill, where, and when. I

can't remember exactly. He gave me a price, and I transferred the money to an offshore account, then he got in touch again asking more questions, and suddenly it just happened."

"Did you ever see the man with the scar again?" I press.

Adam shakes his head.

I couldn't have missed a man matching that description at the party, even though I can't shake a nagging suspicion that I'm missing something.

"How much do they charge for their services?" Freddie asks.

"One million to join the club, then seven million for the kill," Adam replies. A bargain, considering it's a tiny fraction of what he'd gain from Danny's death. "I sent half before and the other half after. They gave me strict instructions to make it look like I was paying for something else."

"Motherfuckers," Callen mutters.

"How can we reach them?" Freddie tries not to sound keen. "Do you still have their number?"

"No," Adam replies. "Every time I called, they used a different number. The first number they gave me expired in a few hours. It makes them untraceable. They told me to only contact them on burner phones and destroy them after each call."

That's a sign of a sophisticated operation. It's not a one-man band but an entire network. An exclusive club of serial killers who cover their tracks. They may be sophisticated, but that doesn't mean we can't find them.

"I swear I've told you everything I know," Adam says. "Now you can let me go. I promise I won't say anything."

Freddie smiles, then looks at me. "You know what to do."

I nod curtly as he leaves.

"What's happening?" Adam asks. His eyes dart wildly to the shut door, then back to me. The realisation that his life is about to end hits him then. "You said you'd let me go."

Adam's said enough. There's no justice in letting another killer walk the streets. We have a duty to protect.

"You're not going anywhere," I sneer, holding up the drill. "This is for Danny, from the Dukes."

"No!" Adam's screams don't affect me. "Please, no!"

On the other side of the room, my phone vibrates on the counter.

"It looks like your girl has finally got in touch, Seb," Callen calls over, peering at the screen. "She wants dinner."

I hesitate as the screw edges into Adam's temple. As much as I'd like to finish the job, the mention of Rose sends blood rushing straight to my cock.

"Would you like to take over, Callen?" I ask.

He nods eagerly and hurries to take my place. I wipe my hands carefully as Adam cries for help. He'll be quiet soon enough.

I text Rose back:

> How about tonight? The Orchard Garden at 8?

"You'll have to run a check on her," Callen says, clutching the drill tightly as it hits Adam's skull. He'll die soon. "Who knows what kind of family she's from? We can't have you dating someone who will cause political outrage. What would your mam say?"

I'm past caring what my parents think. In their eyes, I will always be their greatest disappointment.

Bram shuffles on his feet and tilts his head pointedly towards his backpack.

I raise my eyebrows at him. "You've already done it?"

Bram nods. Damn, he's a good friend. I owe him a pint —well, a non-alcoholic one.

"And she's clean?"

Bram nods, ignoring the bloody display unfolding between us.

"If she's clean, that's all I need to know," I say. "Destroy the files."

Bram tilts his head. *Are you sure?*

"I said, destroy them."

I don't want to get to know her by reading a file. I want to find out about Rose by speaking to her. It's been a long time since a woman intrigued me.

It's hard to get a reservation at the Orchard Garden. The waiting list is months long, but I can get a table whenever I want. There are some perks to being related to the royal family.

"I'll leave you two to clean up," I say. My mood is already brightening. "I have a date to get ready for."

CHAPTER 5

IVY

"Do I look okay?" I turn in circles to examine my appearance and frown at the hugging fabric that leaves nothing to the imagination. "Are you sure this isn't too much?"

"No," Stephanie replies with a dazzling smile. She lounges over her four-poster bed like a goddess. She has the best room in the building. It stretches over an entire floor. "It's exactly too much."

I've never been to the Orchard Garden, but it's meant to be incredible. Seemingly, the reservation list is weeks long. Stephanie gave me free rein of her wardrobe for the occasion. I've borrowed an emerald, green dress that hugs all my curves and pulls in my waist while still giving me room to breathe. What is this sorcery?

I narrow my eyes at the five-inch heels with ribbons tied at the ankles. "Are you sure about them?"

"They match perfectly," she says, then winks, "and they have a blade hidden in the heel for emergencies."

Now she's speaking my language. "I guess they'll do then."

"You're overthinking it," she says, rolling her eyes. "You're going for dinner, not a mission."

A knock on her door startles us both.

"Come in," Stephanie calls.

I spin as Jonathon steps inside. The poor guy had his throat cut and lived to tell the tale. Ironically, it's now his killing method of choice. He's been part of the club for seven years, and he's permanently based in our London HQ. When I first arrived, he helped with my recovery.

"What's the special occasion?" His eyes rake over me, and he makes a low whistle. "Decapitation?"

"She has a date," Stephanie replies smugly.

"You?" His eyebrows shoot up in surprise. "A date?"

I glare at Stephanie. "It's not like I have much of a choice in the matter."

"Have fun," he says, but the sparkle in his eyes disappears as he turns to Stephanie. "Alaric wants a word."

"What's happening?" I ask.

"Nothing that you need to be involved in, Ivy," he says sternly. "We have enough people on this."

"Is it the Dukes?" I ask. They're fast becoming a big pain in our arse. "Have you heard any news about Adam?"

"You're supposed to be taking the night off." Stephanie waggles her finger and throws Jonathon a *shut up, or I'll pop your balls* look that makes him slowly back away. She's scarier than everyone here, including Alaric.

"Come on, Jonathon," I say, batting my eyelashes. "You know you want to tell me."

He sighs in exasperation. "We're searching for Adam's body. We're tracking his phone, and it's on the move."

"Did I not make myself clear enough?" Stephanie growls. Momma Bear isn't happy.

He gulps and raises his arms in defeat. "She'll find out soon enough, anyway."

"They left his phone on?" I ask. "Who does that?"

Spoiler alert, only idiots who don't know what they're doing, unless…

"We assume it's a trap," Jonathon says, voicing what I'm thinking. "But we're going to follow their trail to see where it leads. They may want to lure us out, but we'll be there to catch them at the end."

"They won't know what's hit them," I say with a grin. "I'll cancel the date."

I'm a workaholic who hasn't taken a day off for years. I'll cancel my dinner with Seb if they need me. The club always comes first.

"No," Stephanie insists. "You are going on that date, Ivy. We've got everything covered. I'll keep you posted with any updates."

"Do I have to?" I huff like a child being forced to eat a plate of vegetables. "I—"

"Yes, you're going," she says. "And that's an order from me and Alaric."

As frustrating as it is, I have to follow the rules. An order is final, but that doesn't mean I'm happy about it. I pout and apply a layer of red lipstick, then rub my lips together.

"Fine," I say grudgingly. "But keep me posted, and when you find the motherfuckers, make them regret it."

Jonathon rubs his hands together. "Don't worry, we will."

I guess a date with royalty will provide a distraction from the fun I'm missing out on.

———

I arrive at the restaurant early to scope out the venue from the outside. I circle and count all the exits, familiarising myself with the surrounding streets, observing the flow of traffic, and assessing the risks. I have multiple escape routes if I need them.

The Orchard Garden is small and exclusive. It seats fifty and looks like a conservatory turned ballroom on the inside. Lush vines climb up its walls, while crystal chandeliers hang from glass ceilings and cast reflections from the flickering candles on tables.

"Do you have a reservation?" the snooty girl at the front desk asks. She looks up from her clipboard and scowls. She has a face that could do with a slap. "We don't accept walk-ins."

"I'm here to meet someone," I say, "but I might be a little early."

Half an hour early, to be exact. I want to be first here and get to know the environment.

"What's the name?" she asks in a tone that implies she doesn't believe me.

"Sebastian Montgomery."

"Oh." A flush creeps up her neck, and she flashes me a fake smile. "Of course, Miss Hathaway. Mr Montgomery is already seated. I'll show you to your table."

What kind of psychopath shows up thirty minutes early for a date? Well, one who isn't me, anyway.

We stroll through the restaurant. I recognise famous faces and make a mental note as Stephanie would love to hear about them later. A giant tree is positioned at the back of the room. The trunk appears to be propping up the ceiling. Behind it, I spot Seb's feet. When we turn the corner, he stands as soon as he sees me. The first few buttons of his pale blue shirt are undone, and he's paired it with smart navy trousers.

"Enjoy your evening." The woman practically bows. I resist the urge to roll my eyes. She should have a brown nose from how far it's buried up Seb's arse. "I'll be back to take your order soon."

I reach for my chair as she scuttles away, but Seb stops me. He pulls it out for me like a gentleman.

"I can sit down by myself, you know," I reply in irritation. "It's the 21st century. I'm not incapable."

In fact, I'm capable enough that I could chop his beautiful body into pieces and make sure no one ever finds it again.

"I know you're not," Seb replies, a smile tugging his lips. "But I've been brought up with manners."

I bite my tongue to stop myself from asking about his royal roots. That seems like a subject more suited to after the main course.

"Is that why you're so early?" I ask as he sits opposite me.

"The traffic's always bad in the city," he says, "I didn't want to be late. What's your excuse?"

Oh, you know… making sure I can make a hasty exit if I need to kill someone.

"Yeah, same," I lie.

"Wine?" he offers, gesturing at a bottle of red on the table and a white chilling in an ice bucket. "I got both because I wasn't sure which you'd prefer."

"Red," I say without hesitation.

It's my preferred choice, but it's also unopened. It's better to be safe than sorry. First impressions mean nothing. I learned that the hard way.

"I thought so," he says, gesturing for a waiter to uncork it.

"Good choice, sir," he says before hurrying away.

Seb's shirt rides up as he pours, giving me a glimpse of his toned colourful forearms.

"Nice ink," I comment as he slides the glass across the table.

"You're observant," he says. He has no fucking idea. "My family wasn't happy when I covered my body in tattoos." He's testing me. "I'm sure you've read about them?"

"Who doesn't look up a stranger online before going on a date?" I reply.

That's normal, right? A social media search is a given—not that you can trust the information in an age of catfishes. Seb doesn't need to know my serial killer bestie has run a full background check on him.

He laughs. My lips twitch, too. A perfect body and an infectious laugh? This guy must have girls dropping their knickers every day of the week.

"Then you'll understand that my family is traditional," he says. "They look down on tattoos."

"Why did you get them, then?" I ask. "Surely, they're the last people you'd want to upset, considering they rule the country and all."

"Good question." He sips his wine thoughtfully. "I guess I wanted something for me. Something permanent. Something that set me apart from the rest of them. But I compromised by only getting ink that a suit can cover. It makes unavoidable family gatherings more bearable."

I swirl the wine in my glass. It smells expensive. Rich and fruity, with juicy cherries and a slight hint of vanilla.

I arch an eyebrow and tease, "So, you're the black sheep?"

"You could say that," he replies. His eyes burn into mine. They're doing that thing where they're trying to see right into my soul, but I have my guard up. "But what about you, Rose Hathaway? What is your family like?"

I think of Daisy and the happy memories. Our family cottage by the sea. How she loved walking along the pebbled beach with her beloved and overexcitable border collie, Pippy. How she made the most beautiful artwork… then, the darkness comes.

A smash of metal.

Crunching glass.

Her screams.

My sweet, innocent Daisy sprawled over the ground.

Bloody, beaten, naked.

His laugh.

"Rose?" Seb's prompt brings me back to reality. "Are you okay?"

"Yes, fine," I say, clearing my throat. "I'm an only child, and my parents died when I was younger." The lie flows easily. "But my friends are basically my family now."

That's the thing with lies. You need to stay close to the truth to be convincing. When I crafted Rose Hathaway's identity, I planned everything down to the finest detail. That's what you have to do. It's not enough to come up with a fake birthday. You have to know your horoscope, where you were born, the story behind every pivotal moment in Rose's life, and an explanation for how she got her scars. Rose is two years younger than me. The same age Daisy would have been. It keeps her close.

"I'm sorry about your parents," Seb says. "What happened to them?"

His bluntness takes me aback. Most people don't ask how people died, but his candour is refreshing.

"A car accident," I reply. "It happened in my second year at university."

That's not a lie, but I omit how the real me dropped out to take care of my inconsolable younger sister. It's probably the only time I acted like the big sister. Daisy grew up to be the more sensible one.

"It's hard enough when you're that age," he says, shaking his head in what looks to be genuine sympathy. "Where did you study?"

"York," I lie. I know the place well. It's simple to hack into a university system and falsify student records. The club has the resource to create an entire paper trail. If anyone checked, Rose Hathaway has her whole life documented on record. "What about you?"

"St. Andrews," he replies. Well, duh. That's where all the royals go.

A waitress returns and breaks our conversation to take our order. They have a seasonal menu, and everything is organic. Most of it is written in French, so I'm thankful my time abroad has come in handy.

"We'll both take the ten-course tasting menu," Seb says before I can speak and show off my near-perfect pronunciation. "You won't regret it, trust me."

Trust him? I trust no one. I haven't been able to trust a soul since that night. Alaric and Stephanie are the closest people I have to family, but I can't drop my defences with them fully.

"The ten-course tasting menu it is," I say. My mind wanders to what the others are doing and how it's going with the Dukes. I should be out there with them, not here for dinner, but I smile wryly. "It sounds great."

"How did you get into journalism?" Seb asks. He remembers what I told him last time. Nice. Few men pay attention to what you say the first time, let alone recall it again later. "It must be an interesting job."

"It's what I've always wanted to do," I reply. "I like the freedom it gives me. I've not been back in the UK for long. I've been travelling across Europe for the past five years."

"How does it feel to be back?"

I answer honestly. "It's like nothing, and everything has changed. It's still home, but that's not always a good thing. I like to travel and see different places."

Being busy gave me no time to think. Unfamiliar surroundings keep me on my toes and force me to forget. Since returning to London, my nightmares have started again.

"I understand that," Seb says. "It's the same whenever I visit my family for Christmas. They live out in the country. It used to be my home, but it may as well be on another planet. Whenever I go back, it's like stepping into a time machine." He chuckles. "I'm always happy to get back to the city again."

"Royalty and an investor," I say. "You must have to wear a lot of hats."

"It's not always easy," he says as they bring the first course out. "Although I guess that's what happens when you live a double life."

I understand that more than he knows.

CHAPTER 6
SEB

Her guard is up. I can tell from the way she clutches her wine glass stem a little too tightly and how she carries herself. Something is holding her back. Is she nervous, or is she just not into me?

Speaking to Rose is easy. We've talked about everything and nothing at the same time. I know more details about her, but I'm still no closer to getting to know the real her, which adds to my curiosity. She keeps me guessing, and I like that.

I've been on my best behaviour. Acting like a gentleman, not saying anything that'll scare her away. Breezing over my family, and not ogling her perfect curvy body—which is harder than it sounds. When she got up to go to the bathroom, my cock sprung to life at the sight of her round arse in that green dress. She excites me, and I can't fuck this up.

"I've got this," I say as the waitress brings out the bill.

Rose frowns yet doesn't argue. From her reaction when I held out her chair, it's obvious she isn't a fan of chivalry, but that doesn't mean I'll stop. I want to treat her like a queen.

"Thank you," she says after I make the payment. "I could have paid half."

I'm not sure how much journalists make, but I'd hazard a guess that five hundred pounds would be out of her normal price range for an evening meal.

"It's my pleasure," I say, holding her gaze as her pupils dilate. She's attracted to me, but then she looks away. Fuck. She's resisting. That only draws me in more.

What is it about this girl?

We put on our coats. Despite her struggling, I stop myself from offering to help her with it. She's independent. Well-travelled. She's not used to someone taking care of her. I need to tread carefully.

Rose leads the way out of the restaurant. She swings her hips like she owns the place. Heads turn as she passes, capturing men under her spell. A venomous look from me has them returning to their plates and mumbling apologies to their wives while Rose remains oblivious to how irresistible she is.

"We hope to see you again soon, Mr Montgomery," the host says. "Enjoy your evening."

We step into the cold. It's drizzling, and we take shelter under the building. When isn't it raining in London? Neither of us says a word.

"Well," Rose breaks the awkward silence, "thanks for dinner."

For the first time tonight, her confidence seems to waver.

"The night doesn't have to end yet," I say, then add quickly so she doesn't think I'm a sleazeball, "We could go to a bar for a drink?"

"I really should be—"

I don't know what comes over me. Watching her lips part ignites a primal urge, and I lean in to kiss her. She doesn't push me away. Her lips are soft and send an electric current straight to my cock. No girl has had this effect on me before. Her body bends closer like a flower turning to the sun, when suddenly she jumps back like I've burned her.

"I-I'm sorry," I stammer. "I don't know—"

"Just one more drink," Rose interrupts.

Her blue eyes sparkle. She felt it, too. Our connection. A grin breaks over my face as I slip my fingers through hers and repeat, "Just one more drink."

She doesn't want the evening to end either. We cross the road to a popular bar that turns into a club at night. It's one of my favourites. I can hear the blaring music from outside. She hesitates at the entrance. It's small but bustling. People are packed in like sardines.

"Actually, why don't we go somewhere else?" I suggest, reading her reaction. "My car is just over there." I nudge my head in the direction of a limo, not so subtly waiting nearby. "I have champagne on ice."

She chews her bottom lip. Something is bothering her. "Okay, I just need to call my flatmate to let her know I'll be late."

She takes her mobile out of her bag, except pauses before calling.

"I'll wait for you inside," I say, wanting to give her space. Women like to talk about how dates are going, don't they? She couldn't do that with me loitering around. "And if you change your mind, I'll get my driver to take you straight home. Does that sound like a deal?"

She nods. "Deal."

CHAPTER 7

IVY

don't call Stephanie until he's disappeared into the limo. For someone so rich, he's surprisingly down to earth.

Stephanie picks up on the second ring. "How's it going?"

"He wants to take me home in his limo," I say. There's no way I'm getting into a car without checking the plates. "Can you take the plates?"

"You know I can track your phone to wherever you are, right?" I don't have to be there to know she's rolling her eyes. "Why are you really calling, Ivy?"

"I…"

What am I calling for? Advice? Reassuring words? For someone to tell me I'm not crazy for seriously considering breaking my five-year celibacy for a guy I've just met because kissing him made my stomach flip in a way I've only felt once before?

I remember Freddie. The tall, dark, handsome stranger who made me believe that love, at first sight, might not be a myth after all. The memory is too painful to think about. Our perfect meeting is overshadowed by what happened after we said goodbye. The worst night of my life. The day Spencer set my world on fire and burned it to the fucking ground.

Stephanie's tone is gentle. "It's going well, isn't it?"

"Yeah, he's nice," I grumble. And smoking hot, generous, interesting, intelligent, funny—way too fucking nice for someone like me.

"If you want my advice, not that you're asking for or need it..." Damn, she knows me too well. "I'd live in the moment. You're Rose Hathaway tonight. Do what Rose would do. Tomorrow, you can return to being Ivy. You've been working hard. You deserve to blow off some steam."

"Thanks," I say, looking at the limousine. "But can you take the plates, anyway?"

"Fine," she relents. "What are they?"

I reel them off. She can track my phone, but I like to cover all bases. She taps away on a keyboard in the background.

"No priors," she reads off the screen. "The car is registered to Tim Pope. He and Seb are the only licensed drivers, and Tim's worked for him for years. He's a family man. Nothing to worry about."

That's a relief. Only I'm still on edge. Sebastian Montgomery *seems* perfect. What's the catch? Or am I too busy looking for a problem that I can't see a good thing when it's right in front of me?

"Thanks," I mumble.

"Have fun."

I take a deep breath, strap on my big girl pants, and head for the limo.

You still have time to run, Ive.

I ignore the voice in the back of my head and open the

door to find Seb making himself comfortable on the velvet seats. Soft jazz plays and the twinkling lights on the roof look like stars. There's also a television, mini-fridge, large speakers, and curtains covering tinted windows. I'll never want to take the tube again after this.

"You're just in time," he says, opening the champagne expertly and letting the bubbly mixture flow into two glasses. "One more drink."

"Thanks," I say, sliding along the seat opposite him. Despite it being a huge limo, our knees are almost touching because of his height.

Seb knocks on the screen that separates us from the driver, then turns to me. "What's your address? I'll get Tim to drive us."

I reel off the address to my stooge flat, a few streets away from the Killers Club HQ. Alaric owns many buildings in the surrounding area, which we use as our cover for occasions like this.

I take a cautious sip from my flute and ask, "Are you always this charming on a first date?"

"Actually…" He's hiding something. "This is the first date I've been on in years."

It matches what Stephanie found in the background check, yet I can't be sure he's telling the truth without a lie detector to corroborate his story. Butterflies still flutter in my stomach. Goddamn, his ability to make the walls shrink and make all the background fade like we're the only people around. If he doesn't date, why pick me?

"Neither do I," I admit. "Ever."

He leans back in his seat. "Why do I sense there's more of a story here?"

Seb's good at reading people. Too good. I'm careful,

keeping my expression casual as I shrug it off like it's nothing.

"I move too much," I say, flicking my hair over my shoulder. "I never stay in the same place for long enough."

Another lie based on a truth. That is one reason, though not the only one. Spencer ruined relationships for me forever. After what happened, I vowed to never be in one again. They're doomed to only end in pain.

We pull away from the kerb and join the other flashy cars whizzing around this part of the city. There are so many sports cars we could be in the Grand Prix.

His voice deepens as he says, "I hope you stay in London for a while."

His Adam's apple bobs as he runs his tongue over his lips.

"What about you?" I ask, changing the subject and looking out the window to distract myself from the tingling sensation between my legs. "I thought women would be falling over their feet to date royalty. Are you a crazy serial killer or something?"

He chuckles. "I work too much. There's not much free time in my schedule, and I've not met someone I've wanted to get to know better… until now."

Seb keeps talking while I study the faces roaming the streets. Spencer is likely to frequent this area, so it won't be long until I see him again.

I've taken steps to hide my identity by changing my appearance. My hair is now a fiery red, my nose has a slight bump in it from a bad break, and my jawline is different after having surgery to realign it—another thing I have to thank him for. My skin has a healthy glow from years in the sun, and I've learned to enjoy food again. I lost weight when I was with him too, but I've got my voluptuous curves back. I even wear coloured contacts to change my eyes from brown to blue.

Spencer won't recognise me. Besides, he'll never expect to run into a dead girl.

"Tim knows these streets like the back of his hand," Seb says, bringing me back to the present. "He's been my driver for years."

"Alright for some," I mutter sarcastically before I can stop myself.

"You think I've been brought up with a silver spoon in my mouth," he says. I almost choke on my champagne. "I mean, I have." He smiles. "However I don't take any money from my family. I wanted to make it on my own, so when I left home I never looked back. All I have is what I've built for myself."

He's not saying it to brag but to show he isn't a classic stereotype. He wants me to see he's more than an entitled rich guy.

"Through your investments?"

"Yes," he replies. "I've been lucky. I know that, even though my life isn't perfect."

"Tell me, what isn't perfect about your life?" My voice comes out sultrier than I intended. "You seem to have it all figured out, Sebastian Montgomery."

"I'm on a date with a woman I desperately want to impress, but I'm scared I'm fucking it up," he confesses. I didn't see that coming. "Do you have any suggestions?"

I sip my champagne. Okay, by sip, I mean drain the whole fucking glass.

"One drink," he says. His eyes linger on my empty glass, then he looks outside. "It looks like we're just in time."

We've pulled up outside my building, and my heart sinks. Fuck, I'm actually disappointed.

"It looks like we are," I reply, even as I don't move.

I should get out of the limo, return to the flat, and call Stephanie to find out what's happening with the Dukes, but sitting opposite a sexy guy stirs something else inside me. Or it could be the bubbles talking.

"A gentleman is true to his word." Seb sweeps his blonde hair out of his eyes and reaches for the door handle. He pauses and says, "Have a good night, Rose."

But I'm not ready for the night to end. I slide along the seats, and my knee brushes against his. My adrenaline spikes. I don't like people touching me, but Seb? He's different.

Seb's hand still hovers on the handle. I put mine over it and say, "You may be a gentleman, but I'm not a fucking lady."

Then his lips crash against mine. His hands lose themselves in my hair, pulling my body closer to him. Instinct takes over, and I climb onto his lap.

My fingers fiddle with his buttons for a few seconds. Screw that. I tear his shirt open, sending them flying. Beautiful tattoos cover his chest, and they take my breath away. They're stunning—a black crow, a landscape, and so many details that I could spend hours just exploring.

Seb's mouth, breathy and panting, returns to mine. I sink my teeth into his bottom lip and hang on. He growls as his warm hands caress my back, moving down to cup my arse.

"Fuck," he groans.

He lays me down. The velvet tickles my back as he kisses my neck. I wrap my legs around his torso, hitching my dress up to the top of my thighs and exposing my long stockings.

"Rose," he murmurs, "where the fuck have you come from?"

I dig my nails into his broad shoulders in response and eagerly reach down to undo his belt. His hard cock presses against me, ready and waiting.

I want him. Fuck, I don't just want him. I need him. I need to *feel* him.

He pauses, despite his throbbing cock twitching in my hands. "Are you sure you want to do this?"

I buck my hips impatiently, desperate and chasing the moment. "Yes!"

He moves down my body. The seat is wide enough for the two of us to fit. He parts my legs and kisses up my sensitive inner thighs, but I don't want to be teased.

I need to be fucked. Right fucking now.

"Fuck me, Seb," I demand. "I don't want to wait. I want you."

He tears down my thong with his teeth, baring my smooth pussy.

He growls, "I've been wanting to taste your pussy since the moment I saw you."

He grabs my hips and pulls me onto his face. His tongue is wild and slippery, exploring me with desperate need. My thighs shake as I arch my back and gyrate against him. I forgot how good this felt. Vibrators and my fingers are great, but this? Seb's tongue? This is fucking heaven.

"Yes, just like that!" I cry as his tongue plunges inside me, tasting me, and slurping my juices. Then he moves to suck my clit. I snap my legs around his head to hold him in place. "Fuck, Seb. Yes. Yes!"

I come undone, forgetting we're parked on a busy street and his driver can hear everything. The first wave hits, leaving me reeling, but he doesn't stop. He uses his fingers, stroking my entrance, and keeps going until I gush over him. Only I'm not done yet. I grab his hair and force his head back, so he can look at me.

"I need to fuck you, Seb."

He sits up, his trousers still at his knees, and I straddle him. I moan as I rock against him, rubbing my wetness over his cock, but he's not entering me yet.

"Rose," he gasps, "I don't know if I can wait."

I look into his eyes. "You will."

I slide onto him, taking him an inch at a time. My eyes close, and our wild abandon takes over. Seb's hands are all over me. He grabs my tits, squeezing my flesh, while his teeth nibble on my neck, and he whispers in my ear about how fucking good my pussy feels wrapped around his cock.

I ride him hard and fast. He's big, eight inches at least, and wide, filling me properly. Not even the loud music can drown out the wet slap of me riding him.

"Fuck, Rose," Seb murmurs.

His giant hands grip my arse and force me to slow down. The change of pace shocks me, letting me savour every hot inch of his shaft as I circle my hips.

My eyes snap open as he strokes along my cheekbone gently. I pause while he's buried inside me. Our eyes meet, and we share a moment that's more than fucking. It's deeper than that. My eyes widen in fear, scared he'll see through my act, but then he kisses me. A kiss that steals my breath and makes me forget for a split second that the world can be a cruel place. The ripples of pleasure make me dizzy, and my vision swims.

"You're so fucking special, Rose," he murmurs. "I want you to come all over my cock. I want your pussy to soak me. Can you do that?"

I moan as his cock rubs against my G-spot. "Yes."

And I do. I ride my orgasm out, and he comes, shooting a warm burst of liquid into me. He holds me, pulling me close to his chest, and doesn't say a word.

I shouldn't have ended the evening like this. It's too much of a risk. As soon as I'm sure I can move without passing out, I spring off his lap and pull my dress down. His cum drips down my thighs.

"Are you okay?" he asks sharply, concerned. "Did I do something wrong?"

"I…" I need to get out of here. "I really have to go, Seb."

I grab my shoes from the floor that had been kicked off somewhere in the chaos and jump out of the limo, not worried about cutting my feet on any loose glass on the pavement.

Seb lowers the window and calls after me, "Can I see you again?"

I ignore him and let myself into the building. As soon as I'm inside, I slide down the door and pull my knees up to hug myself. My eyes sting as I remove my scratchy contact lenses and shed Rose.

What did I do?

CHAPTER 8
CALLEN

Our plan is working. They tracked the phone, but they're not stupid. They expected a trap. Unlucky for them, they're hot in pursuit of the decoy… and I'm the best fucking decoy.

I glance over my shoulder, and the wind whips past my face. We're on quiet roads racing through the countryside.

"That's it," I purr, revving my engine. "Let them hear you roar."

A massive car is right up my arse, but being on a motorbike gives me an advantage. I lean forward and hold on tight. I'm about to enter *Fast and Furious* mode. It's been a while since I got this baby up to full speed, and she's begging for it. Let's push her to her limits.

We've learned a lot tonight. The Killers Club has resources and money, that's for sure. They run a sophisticated operation. I'm not sure about the scale, but taking them down doesn't intimidate me. I like a challenge, and they're ruining our business.

I swerve dramatically to the left. My wheels squeal

under the tarmac as I lead the car on my tail in the wrong direction. Meanwhile, Freddie and Bram will have arrived at the Seven Sisters. They'll be pushing Adam's body over the cliffs any second now.

From Bram's digging, we know Adam used to live in that area. He won't be the first suicide at that location. Being heartbroken over a best friend's death is a plausible reason to kill yourself. It won't be long until his bloated corpse washes ashore and the Killers Club finds it. It's a shame I won't be there to see their faces when they do, but you can't have everything.

Bright headlights approach. Yet another Land Rover fills the road. Guns point out of its window.

"Looks like backup has arrived," I murmur.

This is what I live for. Who doesn't want a little excitement? Adrenaline consumes me as they fire. I weave to dodge them. If they're not careful, they'll bury bullets in their friends who are closing in from the opposite direction.

I'm close enough to see the driver in the car ahead. He has a scar on his neck, just as Adam described it. They must have got our message. How do the hunters like being hunted? They think they've got me cornered, but I have an escape plan. I always do. Just a little further…

"Hasta la vista, motherfuckers," I roar as I lean to take a sharp right and cut through the hedges. A turn you'd never see unless you already know it's there.

I cackle as wheels skid and metal crunches together behind me. Sorry, lads. I'd have liked to watch the show, but I've got places to be.

Nights like this give me another reason to have left my old life behind. Saving lives gives you power, but taking them is an act of God. Freddie portrays the Dukes as protectors, but I know who we truly are. Killers. We kill to protect. Protect our clients and ourselves. And me? Well, I'm the Duke of fucking chaos.

I'm still laughing hysterically as I whizz through the darkened lanes. After I've put enough miles between us, I pull over and peel off the first layer of fake plates in seconds. They'll be checking cameras if they're as sophisticated as I think they are. Not that it matters. The plates are false, and I'll be gone before anyone finds me.

When I return to the house, it's three a.m. Freddie's car is in the garage, so dumping the body must have gone without a hitch.

The TV blares from the living room. Seb is sprawled over the sofa, flicking through the channels incessantly.

"You're back early. I thought you were going to get your cock wet," I comment. His eyes narrow as I grin slyly. Winding him up is too fucking easy. "What's wrong? Has it been so long since you got laid that you only lasted thirty seconds?"

Seb's lip curls. He jumps up and launches himself at me, ready for a fight. Bring it on.

"Don't," he threatens in a low growl, squaring up against me and pressing his nose to mine. "Don't say another word."

People say I don't know when to quit, but that's not true. I can tell when they've had enough, but I like to keep going. Pushing limits is one of my many talents.

Naturally, I can't resist saying, "Doesn't she want to see your limp dick again?"

It's a perfectly valid question. Seb roars in anger. He swings his fist, clipping my chin, then comes back for more. This time, his fist lands on my face and splits my lip. I laugh as the taste of iron fills my mouth. I wipe the blood dripping down my chin with the back of my hand. There's nothing like a punch to warm the cockles after riding a bike for hours.

"Do you feel better now?" I ask.

He scowls and slumps into his seat again, grabbing the bottle of whiskey nestled next to him. He takes a swig and holds it out for me.

"I…" Seb starts, then stops. "I like her."

"You've only known her for two minutes," I say, taking a drink. It burns my throat and stings my cut, but I like that. "You need to get out more. There's plenty of prime pink pussy in London who'll bend over for royalty."

"She's different."

Different? No, all women are the same. I don't trust them. Sure, I like to fuck them. Sometimes I even enjoy fucking the same woman more than once, but relation-ships drag you down. They hold you back. They turn your life into a schedule of unwelcome obligations. Men lose part of themselves when they give themselves to a woman… but not me.

"Aye," I say. "She's different until she rips out your fucking heart."

Heartbreak isn't a concern for me anymore. You need to have a heart for it to be broken.

Seb shakes his head, running a hand over his face. Poor bastard has it bad. "You don't understand."

"You sound like Freddie," I warn.

Freddie's still pining over a dead girl he met five years ago. They met one time. He never got his cock wet, but he still visits her grave with flowers every month. He's convinced himself she was 'the one', whatever that means.

The world is filled with billions of people. How is it possible there is one perfect person for each of us? It's bullshit, but Freddie believes it. Unfortunately for him, his 'one' got killed in a car accident the night they met. Talk about bad fucking luck.

"Maybe Freddie's right," Seb murmurs, slurring his words. "Maybe she's the one…"

"Keep dreaming." I snort and slap him on the back. "I'll leave some paracetamol on the side in the morning. You'll need it."

CHAPTER 9

IVY

Steam fills the bathroom as the hot water runs over my skin. The dull ache between my legs is the only reminder it happened. My celibacy is over. But it can't happen again, can it? I scrub my skin until it's pink, but it doesn't stop the tingling from where Seb touched me. His hands… his…

Snap out of it. I throw on the nearest clothes in a hurry. *It meant nothing.*

I snatch the green dress from the floor and stuff it into a bag. I'll need to pay for it to be dry-cleaned before returning it to Stephanie. I won't be able to sleep, so I may as well head to HQ, where I can make myself useful.

After quickly checking the street outside my stooge flat, I set off on the short walk. HQ is an unassuming Belgravian townhouse. Alaric also owns the houses on either side of it. The basements have been combined and consist of three floors.

Stephanie once told me the club has twenty-five agents in total. Twenty-five killers trained to the highest standards. I don't know who, or where, the others are since it's a security risk. But London HQ is where most of us start on our journey.

Everyone knows Alaric and Stephanie. Our boss and his girlfriend. Apart from that, I've only met a few others from my training, including Jonathon and an arrogant set of twins. They like to keep us isolated in smaller groups, even though the club has bases all over the world. Occasionally, I overhear whispers about what's going on outside of my bubble, including talk about a mysterious agent who is known for leaving flowers at crime scenes, but Alaric likes to keep rumours to a minimum. Chances are, the other agents are overseas or dead—well, really dead this time.

All of us are dead, at least on official records. We're ghosts. We shouldn't exist, but we do. Some of us have graves, and some even have families who still mourn our deaths. Alaric gave us a second chance at life, and we took it.

I duck to use the retina scanner at HQ's entrance. High-security precautions aren't out of place on a street like this.

"Hello?" I call as I enter.

My voice echoes through the vast foyer. It's a beautiful house, but all the action happens below ground.

I move to the bookcase, pull out a few special editions, and it slides to reveal an elevator. That'll never get old. I step into the steel contraption and descend into the darkness. When the doors open again, I'm confronted by chaos in our large, open-plan control room. It's modern, with crisp white walls and floors. There are desks, sofas, and multiple screens mounted on the walls, as well as boards with maps and scrawled ideas. This is the hub of the building, with many corridors leading from it.

"I said I'm fine." Alaric bats Stephanie's hand away as

she tries to clean a bleeding cut on his cheek. "It's nothing."

"Hold still," she insists. "You're going to need stitches."

"I'll do them," I offer.

A job like that requires precision. It'll also help to take my mind off my date with Seb.

"What are you doing here?" Stephanie whirls around and points a bloody rag at me in accusation. "You're supposed to be on a date."

"I knew you'd bail," Jonathon says, then winks. "You like breaking hearts."

Years ago, he tried to hit on me. There's nothing wrong with Jonathon. He's a handsome guy, but not my type. Mixing business with pleasure doesn't work unless you're Stephanie and Alaric.

"What happened?" Stephanie presses. "Did you have a good time? Was he nice? Do we need to send someone after him?"

I avoid her gaze. "It went... fine."

"You fucked him," she squeals, making Alaric wince and rub his ears. "That's huge, Ive."

Just like his cock.

"Can we talk about this later?" I snap. "We have other priorities, like fixing the gash in Alaric's face. Is anyone going to tell me what happened?"

Alaric's expression darkens. Despite looking like a terrifying criminal, he's a teddy bear when it comes to the people he cares about. He's been in the business for so long that he rarely gets hurt.

"What did I say?" I ask as he stomps away.

"Ignore him," Stephanie dismisses. "I want to know more about your date. How was it? Was he good?"

Good? My pussy turned into fucking Niagara Falls. I can feel my cheeks heating as my body remembers.

"I've got stitches to do," I say, avoiding her question and hoping my foundation masks my blush. "Alaric, wait!"

The basement floors are split into different zones. A combat area for training, a prison, a morgue, a weapon bank, and a torture chamber—well, duh, for obvious reasons. We also have a state-of-the-art medical room, where I stayed for months when I first arrived.

"So, go over it again," Stephanie says to Jonathon as they trail behind me. "What happened when you caught up—"

I stop in my tracks, wanting all the details. "You found them?"

"We didn't find them exactly." Jonathon scowls. "We tracked the phone to a location. The fucker was on a bike, and he got away."

"He got away?" My jaw drops. We never fail. Now I understand why Alaric is pissed off. "Did you see what he looked like?"

"No," he hisses. "His giant fucking helmet covered his face."

"Woah, touchy," I mutter.

"It was a one-off," Stephanie says. "The Dukes are mavericks. They're like all the other gangs who come and go. We'll find them soon. They're nothing we can't handle."

We try to stay out of gang politics and only get involved if it affects us. The Dukes, whoever they are, have crossed us for the last time. When—not if—we find them, they're dead.

We enter the medical room to find Alaric standing by the mirror, stitching his wound himself.

"I offered to help," I say, crossing my arms. His stitching is uneven and wonky. "You'll look like the Joker."

"I'm fine," he says, wincing, as he pulls the thread through. "Stop fussing. Can't I get a minute of fucking peace here?"

"Leave him to it," Stephanie says. "He's cranky."

"Stephanie." Alaric lowers his voice to a menacing rumble. "I swear I'll—"

"We're leaving," she cuts him off, gesturing for us to shuffle out behind her. She clicks the door shut and then checks her phone. "I'll wait until he's not holding a needle to tell him Adam's body's been found."

"What happened to him?" I ask.

"They threw his body off the cliffs." She rolls her eyes. "How original. It'll be easy to write off as a suicide."

Jonathon frowns. "Our guys found it first, right?"

We have sources inside law enforcement. They may take an oath, but everyone has a price—even those who promise to protect the public. Having people on the inside makes it easier for us to pull the strings and cover-up stories we don't want to get out.

"Uh-huh," she confirms. "Early reports indicate Adam was tortured before he died. He had missing fingers and teeth, as well as an entry wound to the head. It would have been a slow and painful death."

"Who the fuck do the Dukes think they are?" I hiss. Anger builds inside me, bubbling and threatening to explode.

"We'll handle it," Stephanie says, putting her hand on my arm to calm me. Nothing fazes her. "I'm glad you had a good night, though."

"Yeah, I'm glad someone had fun," Jonathon mutters sarcastically, still annoyed about the bastard getting away from him.

If I'd been there, the motorbike would have been flattened and the driver's entrails splattered over the road. The Dukes won't get a second chance again, especially if I'm around.

CHAPTER 10

IVY

Her wide eyes are brimming with terror. An innocent rabbit trapped in the razor-sharp teeth of a ruthless predator. Her white dress is stained red, but she's alive.

"Ivy," she screams and tries to scramble, but he grabs her ankles to force her back. Yet, she still calls for me. I'm the older sister. It's my job to protect her. "Ivy!"

I look up at their faces, trying to make sense of their features. I pinpoint the details, squinting to see past the blurry edges. He has an eagle tattoo on his neck. The one next to him has a wedding ring with a distinct marking. The other has a distinctive scar across his knuckles. I squeeze my eyes shut like the pressing of a button on a camera. I have to remember.

Their laughter cuts through her desperate pleas. She's nothing more than a toy for them to play with.

One turns to the other and asks, "Who wants to go first?"

Vomit rises in my throat, and I swallow it to stop myself from choking. What would his wife say?

No!

Please, no!

Eagle Tattoo steps forward. He's short and stocky. Daisy's smaller in comparison, and he likes that. The sick fucker gets off on the power. Through my tears, I see the boner in his pants.

"Daisy," I croak. "I'm here."

But she's too far away, and I can't move. My cheek presses into the dirt. Spencer's weight crushes me, and my lungs burn with each breath as if I'm being torn apart.

The man kneels beside Daisy and snarls, "You're not going anywhere."

Scarred Knuckles smirks. "Well, not until we're done with you."

I thrash around, desperately willing my body to move, but a sharp blow to my head causes my vision to fade. Spencer's laugh is the last thing I hear before the darkness rolls in…

Fuck! My scream wakes me from another nightmare. Cold sweat drenches the sheets. I can still taste the earth in my mouth, the soil down my throat, and the spine-chilling fear of being utterly powerless.

I stagger out of bed and into the shower. The water is freezing, but I step under it anyway. My chest heaves while the icy spray lashes against my back like a punishing whip. It's relentless, but it anchors me to reality. It reminds me of my purpose and what I'm here to do. Every day is another step closer to finishing my hit list.

They are going to pay for what they've done.

The nightmares used to happen every night. Over the years, they've become less frequent, but since returning to London, they're back with a vengeance. Sleeping pills aren't an option, either. I've tried them, but they give me mind fog, and I have to keep my senses razor-sharp.

I emerge from the cubicle, shivering, and grip the sink for balance. When I look in the mirror, I don't see my reflection. I see his face. The man at the launch party.

The one with the wedding ring. He pulled her ankles and laughed at her. I'm shaking, not from the temperature, but from the blazing hate scorching through my veins.

I return to the room, a spare one in HQ where I stay when I'm here. I pull on a sports bra and leggings. When I feel like this, only one thing will help.

The overhead lights automatically click on as I go to the combat room. The cool marble floor chills the soles of my feet with each step.

The combat area is where we train. It's filled with exercise equipment: a boxing ring, floor mats, and punching bags. I make a beeline for the human dummy on a stand. If I concentrate hard enough, I can see his face. The flesh-coloured dummy morphs into his features, and I take a swing.

My fist pounds into the material. Not bad. I hit again, imagining his teeth rocketing through the air. Another punch. Straight to the throat, making him splutter. Another. Right to the gut. He doubles over, shakily raising his hands in surrender. I keep going, ignoring my screaming knuckles. Again and again.

"Having trouble sleeping?" Alaric's voice comes from out of nowhere.

I spin, panting, as he steps out of the shadows.

"No, I'm fine," I lie. My nightmares returning feel like a regression, but I won't say that—not to the man who brought me back from the brink of death to give me more power than I could have dreamed of. "I want to get some training in early."

"It's okay to trust people, Ivy," Alaric says gently. "Trust is a strength, not a weakness."

I scoff and punch again as it morphs into Spencer's

leering image, desperate to twist his smarmy face out of joint. Just like he did to me.

"I said I'm fine," I repeat, then take a second to catch my breath. "But there's something that will help."

"Your list?"

I narrow my eyes. "How did you know?"

"I made you leave the country for so long for a reason," he says. "You needed time to hone your craft and become the best. When you work through your list, I need to be sure you won't be blinded by your emotions."

"That won't be a problem," I say, turning to high-kick the dummy.

"You've seen one of them, haven't you?"

"Are you stalking me now?" I glare at him. "I'm not one of your marks."

"So you have," Alaric infers and approaches cautiously. "Ivy…"

"I'll give you a matching scar if you're not careful."

He laughs. "Do you remember what I said when I gave you the choice?"

"Of course, I do," I say. How could I forget? The deal we made is what keeps me going.

"Killing them was your reason for living," he says. "I agreed to show you how to do it and let you have your list, as long as you kill on my terms and don't jeopardise the club."

Over the years, I've been tempted to break our agreement. Times when I wanted to say 'fuck the club' and hunt the bastards down, but my training taught me better than that. Alaric is a man of his word, and I owe him—and the club—my loyalty. Without it, I'd be the same weak and pathetic woman who couldn't protect herself or her sister.

"Yes," I reply through gritted teeth. "I remember."

"Good." His eyes meet mine. "I think you've waited long enough. It's time for you to tick a name off your list."

"Seriously?" My voice trembles. "You mean it?"

"Yes, but I need you to do something for me in return."

"Of course," I say. My mind is already racing with ideas about how I'm going to make them suffer and how hard I'll laugh when they beg for mercy that'll never come. "I'll do anything."

"I need you to find the Dukes," Alaric says, "and bring them to me."

That's it? Easy-peasy.

I nod sharply. "Consider it done."

"Good," Alaric says. "Now, who is the first name on your list?"

"Anthony Steel," I reply without hesitation.

The monster from my dream and the man I saw at the party. I learned the names of Spencer's accomplices years ago. Alaric helped me compile my hit list while I recovered from the attack. From my descriptions and with Penelope's help, we identified the three monsters who helped Spencer Bexley destroy my life.

Anthony Steel. Graham Baldwin. Christopher Trout.

Letting them live has been the ultimate test of my self-control, but my patience will finally be rewarded. They all need to be wiped from existence.

"I'll give you Steel's address after you help Stephanie later today," Alaric says. "She's following a lead on the Dukes."

"No problem," I say. The Dukes are a small snack, but Steel is going to be a big fucking meal. "But I want you to know that I'm doing it my way with Steel. I want to take my time."

"Take as long as you need," Alaric says, cracking his knuckles. "I'll make sure the chamber is free."

He turns to leave.

"Alaric?" I call after him, and he pauses at the door. "Thank you."

"Don't thank me," he replies gruffly. "Do your job."

CHAPTER 11
IVY

Stephanie tuts. "Are you ignoring his texts?"

"We're working," I snap. Seb has texted twice today, and I've deleted them both. I don't need any distractions when I have a name to tick off my list, especially when that distraction is a smoking hot royal who has tea parties at Windsor Castle. "Are you going to tell me where we're going?"

We're wearing matching little black dresses. Stephanie's blonde hair is tied in a high ponytail that swishes down her back, drawing attention to the short skirt that barely covers her arse.

"We tracked the movements on Danny's phone," she explains. Her heels click on the paving stones. "For the past year, he rarely went anywhere but home and his office. But when he ventured out, he went to the same bar. I want to see if anyone recognises him, or even better, get camera footage from when he visited to try to ID anyone he spoke to."

"And that should lead us straight to the Dukes," I say.

"In theory," she replies, stopping to reapply plum lip gloss. She holds it out. "Go on, it's your colour."

I take it from her, apply a light layer, and throw her my most murderous smile. "Happy now?"

"I'd be happier if you texted him back," she says, continuing to walk down the street. "Don't you get bored of killing all the time?"

The only boring thing is her stupid questions. She should be pleased I know what my priorities are. Dating is at the bottom of my list, aka never going to happen.

A car slows next to us, its window lowering, and the occupant wolf-whistles. I'm about to tell the creepy perve where to go when I see it's Alaric.

"You're not coming too, are you?" I ask nervously.

Stephanie will attract attention in her gorgeous dress, and I can't let their deadly foreplay scupper my chance of getting Steel's address.

"You two have it covered," he says, crawling along. "But I'll be circling, and Jonathon's down the street if you need backup. Have fun."

Stephanie flutters her eyelashes back. "Not as much fun as I'll have when I get home."

"Get a fucking room," I mutter.

Alaric smirks, ignoring my comment. "See you later."

They make a great couple. He's strict, and her playfulness balances him out, but their PDA makes me want to vomit. Alaric's also fiercely protective. I've lost count of how many bodies are piled up because men got too handsy with her.

"Maybe we should go on a double date?" Stephanie suggests as Alaric revs his engine and disappears. "I'd like to get to know your new prince."

"Not happening."

Stephanie pouts. "You're no fun."

She has the looks of an angel and the brutality of the devil. Alaric calls her his kitty-cat because of how she toys with her prey before putting them out of their misery.

Like the rest of us, Stephanie was close to death when Alaric found her. After beating her to a pulp, her father threw her into a dingy alleyway to die like a street dog. She and Alaric have been inseparable ever since, and he took care of Stephanie's father himself.

"Where is the bar, anyway?" I ask.

Stephanie points at the long line of people snaking around a building. "There."

"Look at the queue," I groan. My dress sits mid-thigh because I'm not the height of a supermodel, but still. We're basically naked.

"We won't have to join the queue," she says smugly, slipping her arm through mine. "Now walk like you own the fucking place."

The street is our runway. Alaric parks opposite, and she blows him a kiss. His grip tightens on the wheel as heads turn in our direction. Yep, it's better he stays outside.

"Head up," she instructs. "Arse and tits out."

"I know how to flaunt it," I snap.

I flick my long hair over my shoulder. We don't walk fast. We take our time as jaws drop and jealous girlfriends screw up their noses at us.

"Hey, there's a queue," a brave woman shouts angrily.

"Oh, we know," Stephanie replies, shooting her a sparkling smile as we cut in front of her to face the bouncer. She runs a red-tipped finger down his chest. "I thought you might help me and my friend..." She leans and whispers in his ear, making his cheeks flush.

I don't want to know what she's promised him.

"G-go right in," he stammers.

"Thank you, sweetie." She holds his gaze, and his blush deepens. "We won't forget this."

I roll my eyes. Stephanie can manipulate men like they're puppets.

"What did you say to him?" I ask as soon as we're inside.

"Watch and learn," she replies, heading straight for the bar.

Despite the long queue outside, it's not heaving. The bar is split over two floors—a trendy cocktail lounge with plush seating as you walk in and a dance floor below that's making my feet pulsate.

A bartender comes to serve us instantly, ignoring a group of men who scowl because they've been waiting a while.

"We may be at work, but it doesn't mean we can't have fun," Stephanie says. "This is your homecoming."

My real homecoming gift will be watching the blood drain from Steel's repulsive face and giving my undivided attention to the other names on my list. I'm saving Spencer until the end.

"Tequila?" I sigh as she plops a saltshaker down and passes me a lime segment. "Really? Aren't we too old for that?"

I'll be thirty next year, and Stephanie is older than me, but she doesn't look a day over twenty-five. Who needs Botox when taking lives gives us an extra boost of vitality?

"You're never too old to party," she says, then smiles. "Come on, live a little. Getting what we want is going to be easy."

Her baby blues are fixed on a bartender who keeps

glancing over while serving other customers. She bites her lip and beckons him closer with her little finger.

"Why did you need me to come with you?" I demand, watching her reel him in like a fish. She has it covered without me.

"I thought it'd be fun," she replies with a devious glint in her eye. "You need to get out more."

Unbelievable. I sprinkle salt on my hand, lick it off, down the tequila, and suck the lime without wincing. I'd have left if I didn't promise Alaric I'd stay.

"I'll look around and monitor the perimeter," I hiss and slam the shot glass down, fracturing it from the force. "Come and find me when you're done."

"Oh, I will," she replies as she leans over to give the bartender a better view of her tits. "See you later."

"I've got a break coming up," I hear him say as I head into the crowd.

Four cameras are positioned in each corner of the bar. I circle to the toilets to look inside—nothing out of the ordinary. The first floor is filling up, so I make my way downstairs into the pit of dancers and pounding music.

If the Dukes are here, I'll find them.

CHAPTER 12
SEB

stand in the shadows, clock-watching and hoping I can leave soon. I'm not in the mood to dance, not tonight.

I check my phone for the hundredth time. Rose hasn't replied. We had the best sex of my life, and now she's ghosted me. Didn't she have a good time? Yes, her sweet pussy gushing all over my face proved how much she did. No one is that good at faking it. Her playing hard to get is driving me insane.

My head aches from the booming speakers, but I sip my drink. Hair of the dog is the best way to recover from a hangover, or so Callen says. He's covering upstairs. This is one of our regular haunts. Somewhere people know they can find the Dukes. We'll have to change our habits soon, though. If the Killers Club are looking for us, it won't be long until they search here.

They've picked the wrong people to mess with. They're hunting the hunters. We're the ones who track people and stop them from becoming a problem. It's what keeps our clients safe. That's our fucking job. Although the Killers

Club finding us is a small worry compared to Rose not texting back.

Maybe Callen's right. Am I going soft? I thought Freddie was crazy to be heartbroken over the death of a girl he met once—well, crazier than his usual criminal mastermind level. I never understood how he felt before, but I get it now. Boy, do I get it…

Since meeting Rose, she's all I think about. I look for her everywhere I go. Even now, red hair swishing through the dancing crowd catches my attention, but I'm being irrational. Rose isn't the only woman in the capital with red hair. Still, I keep watching her.

My heart quickens when the woman pushes past a rowdy group of men and her face turns in my direction. I blink to make sure I'm not imagining it. Motivated perception is real; our eyes can show us what we want to see.

No, it *is* her.

She's really here.

A rush of possessive rage takes over me as another guy's hand slides around her waist to lure her for a dance. My hands ball into fists. He can't touch her. She's all fucking mine.

I storm across the dance floor, leaving spilled drinks and tumbling drunks in my wake. I'm an unstoppable tsunami. Nothing will stand in my way until I reach her.

The man reaches for Rose again, but I'm quicker. I grab his wrist and twist it, making him yelp. His grimy fingers aren't touching her if he wants to keep them.

"It's time you leave," I snarl.

Reluctantly, I drop my hold before I crush his bones. He shudders at my thunderous expression and scampers back to whatever hole he crawled out of.

Rose squints up at me in disbelief. "Seb?"

Her eyes widen in genuine surprise. The darkness makes it hard to see, but my gaze trails down her body as I drink her in. Her tight black dress highlights her shapely thighs and round tits. Fuck, they'd look good with my cock wedged between them. It takes all my willpower not to sweep her into my arms and take her right here.

We both ask in unison, "What are you doing here?"

We can't talk properly over the blaring music. She has to stand on her tiptoes, even in heels, to shout in my ear, "My friend dragged me out."

I smile sheepishly. "Same."

She's holding her phone in her hand and notices me looking at it.

"I'm sorry I didn't reply," she yells, reading my thoughts. "I've been busy."

Too busy to send a thirty-second text? I try to push my doubt away. Maybe I'm overthinking it because my ego's bruised. In the past, I had the opposite problem. Most women were too clingy, and my biggest issue was having to change my number to *stop* them from texting.

"So…" I put my hands on her waist and draw her closer. "You haven't been ignoring me?"

Her body moves against mine to the rhythm. The sway of her hips reminds me of how incredible it felt to be buried deep inside her and how her moans vibrated through my entire body. Why does it matter if she didn't reply? Not everyone acts like an obsessed stalker after one date. She's here now, and her hard nipples pressed against me show she's happy to see me.

The purple strobe hits her face, illuminating her full lips, thick eyelashes, and cute freckle-covered nose with a bump at the top, but there's something different about her…

"I'll be right back," she yells.

CHAPTER 13
IVY

Fuckety-fuck-fuck-fuck!

I leave Seb sporting a semi in the middle of the dancefloor and flee to the toilets. He looked at me strangely, like he was trying to figure something out. Did he notice my eyes? He's never seen me without my blue contact lenses.

I march into the only vacant cubicle. Outside my door, a girl sobs about a loser ex. A group of strangers swoops in to tell her how beautiful she is when she looks like a snotty wreck. Where do these girls come from? They lurk in the shadowy corners of bathrooms and materialise whenever someone has boyfriend trouble or needs a tampon.

I rummage in my bag to find a spare pair of lenses. I pop them in quickly, hoping Seb didn't notice. Even if he did, the light playing tricks could easily explain it away.

What is he doing here, anyway? I'm working. No matter how hard I try, I can't seem to avoid him. Am I doomed to be taunted by the cock I can't have? Sex with Seb was an amazing, mind-blowing mistake. I don't need distractions—no matter how devastatingly gorgeous they are—when I'm focusing on my hit list. It's too dangerous.

The girls continue to offer words of advice that echo in the bathroom.

"Follow your heart…"

"Listen to the universe…"

"It's never too late…"

Pfft, their generic BS doesn't apply to my situation. I tidy up my smudged mascara and send a rushed text to Stephanie to let her know Seb's here.

She replies instantly.

> Job done. On my way to meet your prince
> ;)

Brilliant. Arguing will only encourage her more. I inhale deeply and hold on to it, hoping I can stay calm enough to keep my shit together.

I eat men like Sebastian Montgomery for breakfast. There's no reason for him to make me nervous.

I zhuzh my hair, hold my chin high, and strut out as if I'm an ordinary girl on a night out. Seb is waiting outside and grins when he sees me. A cheeky half-grin that warms me in ways I wish it didn't. How's it possible that he gets hotter every time I see him?

"What's wrong?" I ask him. "Were you afraid I'd run?"

"I needed to be sure you weren't avoiding me," he replies.

Next to him, two girls' faces fall with crushing disappointment. Seb's oblivious to their attention. It looks like they were about to pluck up the courage to speak to him. *You snooze, you lose, ladies.*

"I really have been busy," I say as he slips his hand

through mine. This corridor is quieter than the main floor. I sigh exaggeratedly. "Work's been hectic." That's not a lie. "And my flatmate's going through a breakup." That is a lie, but a believable one. "That's why we're out tonight."

Over Seb's shoulder, I spot Stephanie. She checks out his arse and mimes 'nice'.

"Rose," Stephanie calls, coming over to join us. "I've been looking for you everywhere. You must be Seb. I've heard all about you." She thrusts her hand out for him to shake. "I'm Bethany."

"I'm sorry about the breakup," he says in a sincere tone.

Stephanie slips into character seamlessly. "Fuck him. The bastard was screwing his secretary for months. How unoriginal, right? I found them in his office when he was working late. He had her bent over the photocopier. The bitch faked an orgasm, too; there's no way his tiny dick can make anyone come from that angle."

I arch an eyebrow. She's having too much fun with this. She turns cover stories into Oscar-winning performances.

"You're better off without him," I say, cutting her off before we get a blow-by-blow account of a fictional penis and its misdeeds.

"It sounds like it," Seb murmurs in agreement.

The poor guy doesn't know what to say. It's not the first time Stephanie's left a man lost for words, but she typically likes to gag them.

"Anyway," she says, "I came to tell you I'm leaving."

"I'll come with you," I offer.

"No, you stay here," she insists. "I've found someone to keep me company, and it might get a little wild..." She winks. "If you know what I mean."

Unfortunately, I do. When I used to live in HQ permanently, earplugs were my best friend until her bedroom got soundproofed. She and Alaric are like lions when they go at it.

"So, that's your flatmate?" Seb asks as she disappears.

"Yep," I reply, glowering at her retreating ponytail. "That's her alright."

A smirk dances over his lips. "And you told her about me?"

Out of the entire conversation, how is that what he picked up on?

"I told you I wasn't avoiding—"

He kisses me before I can finish my sentence, taking my breath away. Is his spit laced with a drug that's programmed to transform an assassin into a lusty mess?

"Come with me," he says, tugging my hand towards a fire exit.

I know what I should do. I should make an excuse to leave. I should scope the venue for suspicious-looking people. I should stay away from men with royal blood-lines. Only I don't act on any of my instincts. Instead, I let him guide me, throwing my professionalism out the window because my pussy has other ideas. I blame the tequila.

A brisk breeze hits us as we step into an empty court-yard. The music is vibrating the building, but I can finally breathe away from the mass of writhing, sticky bodies.

Seb pushes me back against the wall.

"Since our date, you're all I've been thinking about." His breath tickles my neck. "And you look fucking incred-ible tonight."

His hands slip up my thighs, sliding underneath my dress. His fingers caress my inner thighs as they make their way up to my heat. How is his touch so addictively good? I moan into his mouth as his fingers stroke my pussy over the wet fabric, while his tongue takes from me with urgency.

I pull away from our kiss breathlessly. "Seb, we shouldn't..."

I gasp as he moves my underwear to the side and strokes along my wet slit. My body surrenders. Now that we've started, we can't stop. His broad shoulders block me from the view of anyone who may come out, yet I can't think about the consequences when I'm blinded by desire.

His enormous palm envelops my pussy, rubbing against my clit as he slides two thick fingers into me. I whine as his pace quickens, plunging his fingers in and out in deep strokes. My thighs tremble, and I struggle to stay standing, but he doesn't stop.

I reach for his fly. His cock is hard, straining at the seams and close to tearing the stitching. I want him to bend me over and fuck me right here.

"This is all about you, Rose," Seb purrs, stopping me with his spare hand. "I want you to come all over my fingers. I want you to come so hard that your sweet pussy soaks me."

I gyrate my hips so he hits the perfect spot. How can he make me this wet so fast?

"Do you like that?" he murmurs.

"Yes," I whimper. "Fuck, Seb. You're—"

I lose the ability to speak as his fingers press against my G-spot. My eyes widen in surprise as I cry out, and my pussy clamps on his fingers. His body pins mine in place, holding me up as I come all over him. Pleasure rushes in crashing waves, and Seb's pupils dilate as I drown him in slippery warmth.

"You look beautiful when you come," he rumbles.

He slides his fingers out of me, shiny from my juices, and pops them into his mouth to lick them clean. Fuck, that's hot.

"You're right," a Scottish voice chimes in from the shadows. "She does look beautiful when she comes."

CHAPTER 14
SEB

"Callen!" The sweet taste of Rose's wetness on my tongue turns to bitter rage. "You were watching us the whole time?"

Rose stumbles as she pulls her dress down in a hurry. She crosses her arms over her chest. "You know this perve?"

"Hasn't Sebastian told you about me? I'm Callen. We're the best of friends." A sly grin spreads over his face. Yeah, if his definition of best friends means wanting to kill each other. He's loving every minute of this. "We live together."

"Right now, you'll be lucky if I don't knock you out," I spit.

Rose's jaw drops. "You live with *him*?"

Not by choice, I want to add. Callen is the newest Duke. He joined us a year ago and had to complete several trials to prove his worth. Before that, he was a nomad, riding around the Scottish Highlands and causing carnage in Edinburgh. Freddie sees his skills as an asset, but that doesn't stop him from being a liability.

"And we share everything," Callen taunts. "Kitchen pans, the bathroom, even pretty girls…"

Fucking liar.

"She's mine, Callen," I sneer through gritted teeth.

Oomph. I stagger back as Rose's small hands slam into me, pushing me away roughly. Where did that come from? She winded me. I look down, clutching my chest. Her thunderous expression tells me I've fucked up. Badly.

"I'm *yours*?" she demands, arching an eyebrow. Her body language has changed completely. I don't need to psychoanalyse her to know she's furious. "I'm not your fucking property."

"Rose, I didn't mean—"

My inner protector came out, and my words came out wrong. All I want to do is keep a monster like Callen away from her. Now she's forgotten all about him, and I'm the target of her anger.

Her eyes narrow. "I don't belong to anyone. I'm not yours, or anyone else's."

Callen snickers. He leans against the brick and watches the show unfold. If he's not careful, he'll get a black eye to match his split lip.

I fumble, trying and failing to justify my stupid comment. "I didn't mean it to come out like that."

"We've only been on one date," she snarls, shutting me down with a withering look. "You're not my boyfriend."

She's right, though her words puncture my heart like a spray of bullets. Why does hearing it hurt so badly? We're not official, but fuck… her cold indifference leaves a void between us like I'm missing a limb. I can't lose her. I won't.

"She's feisty." Callen steps in and lets out a low whistle. "I like her already."

The bastard's trying to get a rise out of me, sensing I'm

on the edge of exploding. My whole body shakes as he saunters to where Rose is standing, wearing a smug smirk that makes women melt. He looks like a biker with shoulder-length sandy hair and a beard—the kind of guy who should come with a warning label. I take a deep breath and battle my overwhelming urge to step between them. If I do, that'll only prove to Rose I'm a possessive psycho, and she'll never want to see me again.

"I couldn't give a flying fuck if you like me," she snaps. Maybe she's immune to his bad-boy charm. She frowns as she looks at him properly for the first time. "What happened to your lip? Did someone find you peeping through their window, or did your massive ego punch you in the face?"

"You can thank your boyfriend for my extra rugged good looks," Callen replies. He grins at me. "You were right about her, Seb. She's special."

My stomach churns. Callen can't take an interest in her. Yes, he's a Duke—but he's also a twisted motherfucker. A genius with deadly impulses that he can't control and zero morals. Rose is nothing like him. She doesn't belong in our world, and she's been the first good thing to come into my life for years. Is it so wrong to want to keep her to myself?

"I'm leaving," Rose hisses, knocking into Callen's shoulder as she barges past. "Alone."

"Rose, I'm sorry," I call after her, but she slams the door in my face.

I step towards Callen.

"What did I do?" he asks innocently. "I wanted to meet the girl you're crazy about."

My nostrils flare. "You—"

He wags his finger to stop me from talking. "You

slacked off to get your fingers wet on the job. What will Freddie say if he finds out?"

"I'd keep your mouth shut if you don't want a broken jaw," I threaten.

Callen chuckles. "Promises, promises."

CHAPTER 15
IVY

storm through the streets. If my heels were pickaxes, they'd leave cracks in the stone.

A group of men wolf-whistle in my direction, thinking it's a compliment. I shoot them a menacing glare. They laugh nervously and call me a frigid bitch, but something about me makes them uneasy. I can tell from how quickly they hurry in the opposite direction. They can't put their finger on why, but their basic survival instincts kick in. Maybe guys subconsciously pick up on the aura of a woman who isn't afraid to tear their testicles from their bodies. If I wasn't so good at my job, I'd break their necks.

My phone buzzes, but I ignore it. I don't want to read Seb's apologies. *I'm his?* I don't think so. We hardly know each other. Possessiveness is toxic. When Spencer said it at first, I thought it was sweet and proved how much he liked me, yet look how that turned out. No one owns me. Plus, his housemate wanking off in the shadows? It's fucking creepy, even if the guy—Callen—is sex on legs in a rough and ready way.

Jonathon's car is waiting down the street. As I climb

inside, I slam the door behind me, making the car rattle. He winces from the noise.

"Bad night, huh?" he asks. "Stephanie said you might be late."

"Just drive," I growl.

There's only one way I'm going to satisfy my urges. Jonathon knows better than to press me again, and when we arrive at HQ, I order him to stay in the car.

"But—" I glare at him, a signal that I'll castrate him if he argues. He relents and huffs, "Fine, I'll stay here."

I need a getaway car and driver.

"Alaric? Hello?" I yell as soon as I'm in the foyer. "Alaric!"

I head to the bookcase, assuming he's in the basement, when the stairs creak behind me.

"This better be important, Ivy," Alaric roars from the top of them.

He's topless and wearing joggers. Stephanie peers around him with bed hair.

"I want Steel's address," I demand.

"Right now?" He checks his watch and scowls. "You need to plan."

"You know my best work happens spontaneously," I rebuff. "I'll bring him back here."

He considers my offer, weighing up the risk I pose and how blue his balls are going to be if he argues. Stephanie strokes his shoulder to lure him back to bed. She knows what she's doing. Alaric is the boss, but she's the one who gets the final say.

"Okay, okay." He caves as Stephanie whispers something dirty in his ear. I'll thank her later. "I'll text you the address, but bring backup in case things go wrong. I wouldn't say yes if Steel didn't live alone."

"Understood," I say. "Jonathon's already waiting in the car."

I have a renewed spring in my step as I raid the weapon bank. I hum as I put everything I need into a suitcase: rope, cuffs, knives, and syringes filled with a paralysing agent. My hand hovers over a gun, but I decide against it. They're no fun. Bullets are messy and make it way too quick. He deserves my complete care and attention. Besides, knives are much more personal.

I skip through to the torture chamber, swinging the suitcase, and quickly check everything is ready. All the instruments are laid in a neat line waiting for me. Perfect. Now all I have to do is dress for the special occasion. I swap my dress for tight-fitting black cargo pants, a belt with all the necessary tools, and a faux leather jacket.

When I return to the car, Jonathon is miming along and thrashing his head to Ash and the Basilisks. They're his favourite American metal band, and he's low-key in love with Ash. I mean, who isn't? It's no surprise she has three masked hotties who worship her. Lucky bitch.

His eyes light up at the sight of my outfit and the silver suitcase. My kidnap kit. "Who are we gutting?"

I give him the address and add, "This kill is mine, not the clubs'. You can help me take him back, but that's it. Got it?"

He understands instantly. We were all chosen to join the club because of our violent pasts and brushes with death. Jonathon's ex's overprotective brother went on a rampage after Jonathon broke up with her. He cut Jonathon's throat despite knowing his darling sister broke Jonathon's heart by screwing his best friend. The point is, we all have a hit list. Where's the fun in being a ghost if you can't haunt a few people from your past?

"Let's go," he says, hitting the accelerator. "His flat isn't far away."

When we pull up outside his building, the lights are off. Thankfully, Steel's flat is on the ground floor.

I grab the thermal binoculars from the glove compartment and do a check. "Bingo." I grin at the red heat map around a stationary figure. "He's sleeping and all alone."

Jonathon pulls cotton gloves up to his elbows and hands me a pair to do the same. They're a forensic counter-measure, but our prints being found don't matter when Penelope can wipe any evidence in a few clicks. Besides, no one will suspect a dead person of murder.

"It's time to collect," he says gruffly. No one wants Steel dead as much as I do, but Jonathon saw what Spencer and his men did to me. He watched me struggle to rebuild my life and wants them to pay for it. "Do you know which flat is his?"

"Flat two. Second door on the right."

"Perfect," Jonathon says, flicking a switch hidden under the steering wheel. "The disruptor's on."

I'm not clever enough to understand how it works. Essentially, the vehicle becomes a weird signal jammer that messes with any nearby technology. If people check their CCTV footage after our arrival, all they'll see is static.

"It's go-time," I say.

We approach Steel's flat. It's an affluent area, which works to our advantage. Many of the houses are owned by bachelors or sit empty because their occupants are holi-daying abroad to escape the cold. Poor Anthony will soon be wishing he went with his pals to Seychelles.

With a few taps on his phone, Jonathon hacks into and disables the mechanism on the outer door, so we get inside without a hitch. We head to Steel's flat, and I snicker at the keypad requiring a code for entry. Idiot. People think it's more secure than a key, but anyone can get inside if they have the technical expertise. They make our job easier... and quieter.

I twist the door handle after Jonathon does his magic, bloodthirsty excitement building, and lead the way. Snoring comes from behind an open door. I slink through the gap into his bedroom. He's sprawled over the bed—mouth wide open, snuffling like a pig, covers half thrown off. I place the suitcase on the bed, and the pathetic sack of shit stirs as it clicks open.

I grab a syringe and watch the rising and falling of his blubber for a little longer. For a monster who picks on people that can't defend themselves, it's fitting to take him when he's defenceless. I puncture his neck with the needle and inject the clear substance. I'm giving him a double dose as an extra precaution. When Steel wakes, he will find himself in a living nightmare.

I check my watch and start counting down each second until the drug takes effect. Two minutes feel like an eternity after waiting years for this moment.

"All done," I say to Jonathon, who loiters in the doorway.

Steel's eyelids flutter at my voice. He tries to move, awkwardly rocking on the spot, but his muscles seize. His eyes snap open in terrified confusion. He can see, feel and hear what's happening, but his body is frozen.

"Are you going somewhere?" I taunt him. My laughter fills the room. "Too fucking bad."

Jonathon steps from the shadows. "Let's get him in the car."

Carrying him will be a challenge, as well as a risk for others to see. Our best bet is to drape his arms over our shoulders and make it look like he's had a few too many. Anyone peeking through their curtains or driving by will think he's another drunk guy who doesn't know his limit.

"On three," I say. We get in position to hoist him off the mattress. "One, two…"

We haul him from the bed, forcing him upright.

The night Spencer and the others destroyed my life, this man terrified me. But now I'm a phoenix rising from the ashes. Killing him won't bring Daisy back, but it'll make me feel better…

CHAPTER 16

BRAM

Callen and Seb's bickering floats down the hallway. Freddie and I exchange a knowing look. Their competitive spirit brings out the worst in each other, and they argue more than a married couple. They're always rowing over something, whether it's who can down a pint or who can draw a gun the fastest.

While they've been out, we've enjoyed the peace. I scoured the dark web for any mention of the Killers Club, and Freddie researched new weapons to add to our growing collection. He's an expert. After he left the Met, he spent time overseas selling them. That's how we met. Upgrading our arsenal is a good idea, especially with assassins targeting us. We have to be at the top of our game.

Seb bursts into the living room like a blistering inferno, and Callen swaggers in after him. The relaxed atmosphere vanishes instantly. Seb's furious. I can tell from his red face, tense muscles, and the way his entire body shakes like a nuclear reactor about to blow. What did Callen do this time?

Seb spits words like fire. "I don't know what you were thinking when you hired him."

He should know better than to give Callen a reaction. Callen loves getting under his skin and provoking him. When he's in good form, Callen's a joker who can lighten the darkest mood. But, at his worst, he's infuriating enough to drive a nun to violence and would end up with rosary beads wrapped around his neck if he spent a few weeks at a convent.

Freddie glances over the top of the book he's reading. "What happened?"

Freddie is the voice of reason in the chaos. He's the balancing force that binds the Dukes together. He recruited us for our unique skill sets, and his word is final, even when we don't agree.

I lean back in my chair to watch the drama pan out. Believe it or not, being unable to talk has benefits. I communicate in other ways and notice signals other people miss. Seb jokes that I'm a human lie detector, which isn't far from the truth. When you read micro-expressions as well as I can, you'd be surprised at how often people lie.

"He..." Seb is too consumed by his emotions to express himself through words. Instead, he uses the other language he knows best. Violence. He roars and kicks the wall in frustration.

Really? I raise my eyebrows as he grunts in pain. *Did that help?*

The exposed brick walls will break his toes before he does any damage. The three-storey townhouse we call home is industrial and has an open-plan design. It has slick white and black furniture with exposed lighting and copper piping that has no purpose, apart from looking cool. The furnishing is minimal, only containing the basics, meaning we have fewer things to clean and break, which is essential when four men with temperamental moods live under one roof. Despite the challenges of sharing a house, that doesn't affect our work. The Dukes are a unit. One for all, and all for one. Through the good, bad, and fucking crazy.

Freddie, our boss, is the mastermind behind the operation. He's cautious and calculating but charming… when he wants to be. He brings capital, experience, and an unrelenting desire to be—and pushes us to be—the best.

Seb is his number two. If Freddie is a German shepherd, Seb is like a mischievous puppy. No matter what he does or how much trouble he gets into, people love him, anyway. But he's not stupid. Seb's creative and isn't afraid of taking risks, which is how he built his fortune. He's also well-connected in the right circles and knows how to win a fight.

Callen is the Duke's maverick. You never know what to expect from him. He's a genius ex-surgeon with an inflated ego who hides a dark side and a hunger for blood. But he has just the right amount of humanity to stop him from becoming a full-on monster, even if he sometimes crosses the line.

Then there's me. In spite of my appearance and being the biggest of all the Dukes, I'm a computer geek at heart. Nowadays, I prefer not to get my hands dirty. Killing people was normal during my former army days, but those days are over. I learned from the past, and still keep working to make better choices, even when trouble has a nasty habit of finding me.

A familiar whine comes from the kitchen, and I move to let our beautiful border collie, Pippy, in. She is the honorary fifth member of the Dukes, and we all adore her

—even if she has a ridiculous name and demands to be walked for hours. She may be Freddie's dog, but she's captured all our hearts.

Freddie yawns. "Did you meet any potential clients at the bar?"

Pippy follows me back to my spot, nuzzles my leg, then rolls over to demand a belly rub.

"No," Callen replies. "We had a quiet night, apart from meeting Seb's new girlfriend."

"Her name's Rose," Seb hisses.

"He's only mad because they had their first lover's tiff," Callen teases.

Seb glares at him. "No thanks to you."

There's more to this, except he doesn't elaborate.

"You arranged to meet her tonight?" Freddie asks, his tone dripping with disapproval. He's a reasonable boss, but he has high expectations. The Dukes come before anything else. "Is this girl going to be a problem, Seb?"

"No," Seb lies. Interesting. I've never seen him act like this with a woman before. What's so special about Rose Hathaway? "I didn't know she'd be there. I couldn't ignore her without arousing suspicion. We agreed I need to find someone to be my cover, remember?"

Seb's family keeps putting pressure on him to attend more royal functions. Now that he's thirty, they've compiled a long list of potential matches for the city's most eligible bachelor. After seeing their suggestions, I also see the benefit of keeping Rose around.

Freddie ignores Seb and turns to Callen for his opinion. "Is she going to cause us issues?"

"No," Callen replies. Why is he lying? Now I'm really curious about what's so damn special about her. "She's just a gash to get his dick wet."

Seb grinds his teeth but keeps his cool. If Freddie wasn't here, Seb would likely string Callen up from the copper pipes and leave him hanging.

Freddie nods, but his expression turns stormy. "Don't let it happen again, Seb. The Dukes come first."

Seb nods. "Always."

Although, I'm not sure I believe him…

CHAPTER 17

IVY

"You might be wondering where you are…" I drag my words for effect, trailing my hand along the steel bench where he's strapped down. "Or who I am."

We're alone.

Having free rein in the torture chamber is a treat, and I plan to make the most of it. A layer of sweat covers Anthony's greying skin. Poor diddums isn't enjoying the role reversal. His chest jumps with the thumping beat of his heart. I can almost hear it slamming against his ribs, ticking like a bomb about to explode.

"How about now?" I slam my hands on either side of his ugly face and loom over him. "Do you recognise me now that you've had a closer look?"

My nose wrinkles at the smell of his rancid breath as his eyes stare at me blankly. I laugh hysterically, spraying him with my spit. He doesn't know who I am. That's how little my sister or I meant to him. He can't even remember my fucking face.

"Let me remind you," I snarl.

Before Penelope wiped our existence from the internet and Daisy's belongings were disposed of, Alaric set aside one photograph for me. The photograph never leaves HQ, although I retrieved it for tonight. It's a special occasion, after all.

"Do you remember now?" I thrust the image into his face, but he squeezes his eyes shut. My voice reverberates off the walls as I yell, "Look at her!"

His eyelids open. My stomach churns as he visually violates her. He doesn't deserve to look at her, but he has to know why he's here. A flicker of recognition crosses his previously vacant gaze. *There.* A strangled noise comes from the back of his throat. He knows.

"Do you remember her face now?" I ask. "The face of the girl you killed."

I took the picture on my last visit to see her. A rare weekend when Spencer let me out of his sight. We took Pippy for a walk along the pebbly beach from Aldeburgh to Thorpeness, stopping to eat chips and getting ambushed by seagulls on the way. We sat at the lake to watch the rowing boats, and she asked about the bruises on my arms. I lied and told her I had fallen.

"Did you think I was dead too, Anthony?" I move the photo out of the splash zone and keep talking as I put on gloves. "Unfortunately for you, I'm back from the grave. But my sister wasn't so lucky."

He loses control of his bladder and piss soaks through his trousers. It runs off the bench, leaving a steaming puddle on the floor.

Drip.

Drip.

Drip.

"Ruining my heels won't stop me," I say as my fingers close around the hilt of a knife. "You can't escape. There's nowhere to run, and I'm going to show you the same mercy you showed my sister."

I position the blade under his eye. I slide it down his cheek, neck, and chest. It's sharp enough to slice through his top like butter and leave a deep gash behind. Tears fill his eyes. He can cry me a fucking river, but the only liquid I want to see is blood.

"Do you think crying is going to help?" I mock. "Did her tears stop you? Do you remember what you did when she cried and begged for you to stop? You laughed. You treated her like she was nothing!"

He shuts his eyes again. My patience is wearing thin, and I drop the knife. The bastard breathes a sigh of relief, but it'll be short-lived.

"If you won't look at me," I warn him, "I'll have to make you."

I position metal speculums on both of his eyes to prise them open. I'll use a razor blade to slice off his eyelids, but that'll come later.

I bend, wanting him to feel the terror that comes from death breathing down your neck, and whisper, "Do you think she enjoyed you panting on top of her?"

I head to the bench and select another knife, bigger than the last. I sharpen it, relishing the *snikt* sound it makes.

"You were quick when you raped her." My nose scrunches at the sight of his soggy crotch. "But I'm not like you. You'll be pleased to hear it takes me a long time to feel truly satisfied." I run my tongue over my lips. "True pleasure can't be rushed."

I cut his pyjama bottoms from his body and scoff at his

shrivelled dick. His balls have almost disappeared into his body. I run the blade along his tiny shaft. He whimpers—well, as much as he can without moving his lips. Another reason why the sedative is my new best friend.

"I could cut it straight off," I ponder. Alaric told me about a female gang leader in the States. She's cut off more cocks than anyone can count. Her name alone—Candy Cane—makes men tremble. "But I have a better idea."

I hum as I grab a nail gun. If his paralysis worsens, I want to ensure he doesn't go anywhere. The cuffs on his wrists and ankles are foolproof, but I like to be thorough. I stretch his wrinkly skin and laugh as I nail his balls to the bench. Five in each—I'd do more if they weren't bite-sized raisins. It's a pity I don't have Candy's number. I think she'd like to see my masterpiece.

"Have you ever thought about getting your cock pierced before?" I ask. "Some women say it's more plea-surable. Only you've never cared about that, have you? Women won't sleep with you, so you have to take what you want instead."

My phone vibrating causes my voice to trail off. I glance to see a message from Seb.

> I'm sorry for what I said. I didn't mean it.
> Can we talk? Please?

Eurgh. Steel is going to feel the brunt of my frustration. When I've finished with his cocktail sausage, it'll look like a pincushion. He'll never get an erection again, not that he'll have the chance to.

Steel murmurs something through his pressed lips. They're hardly moving, but I listen closely to hear him say, "Kill me."

"Oh, I will," I promise, flashing him a dazzling smile. "But not yet. I'm having too much fun, taking my time to appreciate every inch of you." I glance down. "Or just the one inch from the looks of it."

Where do I start? My options are limitless. But looking at his bleeding slug is making me want to heave, so I'll come back to that later.

"You all left us to die in that ditch," I say as I pull fabric from my pocket. I wrap it tightly above his elbow. That'll keep him alive for longer. "My physical body didn't die that night, but my soul? You smashed it into smithereens, and that's exactly what I plan to do to you. I'm going to cut you into tiny pieces so no one can put you back together again."

What can I say? Humpty Dumpty is my favourite nursery rhyme.

"Please," he breathes. "Kill me."

Sheer fury consumes me as I force open his locked jaw. I reach for my special scissors. Muscle is the same as thick rubber to cut through, but these medical-grade beauties are designed for the job.

"Did you expect me to ask for consent? Too bad," I sneer, squeezing my fingers together and snipping to silence him forever. "You never asked for her permission."

His stare glazes over. It's a good thing I have a dose of adrenaline at the ready. I plunge it into his chest, reawakening him. He's not losing consciousness on my watch. His pain doesn't come close to the crippling agony of losing Daisy. I need him to *feel* what it's like to be ripped apart.

I've spent years perfecting the art of removing a victim's limbs while keeping them alive for as long as possible. When I'm finished, his body parts will rival a museum exhibition.

And the best thing is, I'm only getting started. One name down. Another three to go.

CHAPTER 18

BRAM

Seb hands me one of five giant bouquets and a card with an address on it. The rest of the flowers are lined up by the door. How badly did he fuck up to justify spending five hundred pounds on roses?

"Can you drop these at her house?" he asks. "I'm meeting a client with Freddie, otherwise I'd go myself."

I cock my head to the side. *What's in it for me?*

"A favour."

I raise my eyebrows. *You're going to have to do better than that.*

"Fine." Seb sighs in exasperation. He pulls a stack of twenties from his wallet and slaps them onto my open palm. "Better?"

That'll do.

Seb peers at his shiny Rolex, a recent gift from the father he rarely sees. "I've got to go."

Freddie's waiting in the car outside and beeps the horn on cue, as Seb hurries to join him. I don't know who they're meeting, and I don't ask. Freddie knows all our clients. I do what I'm told and prefer it that way. I don't want to make any big decisions.

"Who are these for?" Callen saunters down the stairs, plucking a note card from the bunch and shaking his head. "Seb's got it bad. How about I help you deliver these? We can stop at the pub on the way back for some scran."

I cross my arms.

Seb won't like Callen knowing where his new girl-friend—or whatever the fuck they are—lives. But Callen's a tight arse, and I'll take a free meal when I've got no other plans.

I nod. *What can go wrong?*

I check her building on a map first. A habit before setting off on any journey, even one as menial as this. Rose lives on a nice street, too nice for a struggling journalist to afford. After running a check and reading her file, I bet she inherited money when her parents died.

"I'll drive," Callen volunteers.

I snatch the keys from his fingers. *No, I'll drive.* He got caught by two speed cameras the last time he got behind the wheel of a car.

"Fine," Callen agrees, "but I call dibs on the music."

I soon regret my decision to bring him with me. He blares out 80s Rock for the entire journey. When I park, I glare at him as he reaches for the handle. *Stay here.*

He holds up his hands with a relaxed smile that makes me suspicious. "I'm not going anywhere."

I pass through the gate and climb the steps to her front door. Her name is written next to flat number one, so I ring the buzzer. No answer. I jab it again and again. Nothing. She mustn't be home.

Fuck it. I leave the flowers on the ground, having to make two more trips back to the car. They fill the entire doorstep and the three steps below it. Talk about overkill. Seb didn't give specific instructions to deliver them by hand, so it's not my problem if someone steals them.

"No one home?" Callen infers.

I narrow my eyes as I buckle my seatbelt. *What do you think, genius?*

We're only driving for a few minutes when Callen points out the window. "Wait, slow down."

I crawl past a redhead with a fantastic body. A man walks by her side. He's tall and handsome, but in an *I wouldn't trust him with my girlfriend* kind of way. There's something else too. A distinctive scar across his neck. How many people have a scar like that in London?

"That's her," Callen says. "Rose."

Wait, what?

"Seb's girl," he elaborates. "The one we just delivered flowers to."

I swipe my hand over my neck in a cutting motion. If he stops checking out her arse for two seconds, he'll see Seb's latest layover is the least of our fucking problems.

"Shit." Callen straightens in his seat. "Yeah, that's the bastard I saw that night."

We watch them head into a pub on the corner. They're chatting like old friends. How do they know each other? Does she know the man she's having a drink with is connected to a mysterious network of assassins? Will she be his next victim?

I tap buttons on the screen in the middle of the dash, bringing up the telephone and finding Seb's name.

"What do you want?" Seb asks abruptly on the second ring. His voice comes through the speakers. "Freddie's just gone inside. I'm busy."

"Yeah, busy being a guard dog." Callen snickers. "How

would you feel if we told you that your pretty girlfriend is having a drink with another man?"

Seb is silent, then turns on me. "Bram, I thought you were going alone."

I shrug, even though he can't see me.

"I thought you'd be interested in how her date has a scar on his neck," Callen says. "The same man Adam described before we put a drill through his head and who tried to push me off the road."

"Follow her," Seb orders without hesitation. His voice turns into a low, menacing growl. He isn't messing about. "Take her home and bring him to us."

"Does this mean you're happy for me to talk to her now?"

"Fuck off, Callen." Seb scowls. "Whatever happens, make sure she's safe. She's the priority."

"Don't worry, Romeo." Callen reaches for the gun tucked into his waistband. "I'll save your Juliet."

"Make sure he doesn't do anything stupid, Bram."

I grimace. With Callen, that's easier said than done…

CHAPTER 19
FREDDIE

pace Spencer Bexley's hallway. His townhouse is like a labyrinth. I know who he is. He comes from a filthy rich family who owns a weapons manufacturing company. Spencer has taken over from his father and a line of Bexleys before him. Spencer accepts a big paycheck for doing very little, but he's known to do dirty deals on the side. But what I don't know is why he reached out to the Dukes to arrange a meeting.

I check my watch. It's been twenty-seven minutes since his housekeeper let me inside. If it gets to thirty, I'm leaving. I stop to examine a painting on the wall. It depicts a smiling woman, yet her frozen eyes and smile are unnerving, like she's hiding a dark secret.

"It's an original." A man steps from the shadows. He holds out his hand. "You must be Frederick James."

I keep my arms pressed to my sides. He's a few inches shorter than me, with short brown hair and icy blue eyes. He would have been good-looking in his youth with his dimples and charming allure, but his looks are fading as years of partying are catching up with him. Everything he's wearing, from his dapper suit to his watch, costs more than a decent car.

I dislike Spencer instantly. It's not just his air of self-entitlement—that's a common trait with our clients—but there's something sinister about him. But my opinion doesn't matter. All that does is whether he can afford our fee.

"Thank you for the invitation," I reply coldly. "I don't like being kept waiting."

"Point taken." Spencer chuckles. Maybe this is a test. "Why don't you follow me to the drawing room?"

Spencer's leather shoes squeak as he leads the way. I note the oak-floored winding corridors, oil paintings, and animal heads mounted as trophies—all the fanfare you'd expect from a member of the pompous British elite.

My skin crawls the deeper we get into the building, and I can't shake the feeling we're being watched. I cast a quick look over my shoulder to see a door propped open ajar. A pair of eyes look back at me through the darkness. But when I blink, they're gone. I mentally shake myself. Probably nothing more than a trick of the light. This place will be crawling with cameras, and someone will be following our every move.

"Nice place," I comment as we pass a grand piano that I'm certain he's never played.

"Thanks," Spencer says, holding open a large door almost as tall as the ceiling. He pauses. "After you."

"No," I say, bowing my head. It's common sense to never go into an unfamiliar room first and always to be positioned closest to the exit. "I insist."

Spencer's fake smile reveals perfectly straight teeth as

he enters. The drawing room is more like a library. Original uncracked spines line the walls, and green Chesterfield sofas are nestled in reading nooks. There's a grand fireplace and a desk with a high-backed chair resembling a throne.

"Drink?" Spencer asks. His type doesn't do business without one. He opens the globe drinks cabinet to reveal a selection of the world's finest spirits. "What's your poison?"

Several chemicals spring to mind, but I reply, "Whiskey."

"Same as me," Spencer says, decanting the amber liquid into glasses and handing me one. He swirls his around the crystal and inhales deeply. "It's one of the last bottles from Skeller Rock, before… well, you know the rest."

Everyone's heard ghost stories about the haunted island where a mass murder occurred. It's long been closed to the public, but rumour has it that visiting sends people to the brink of madness. Not that I believe it. Ghosts don't exist. There is no coming back from death.

He watches closely as I sniff. You can smell the rough high tides of the North Sea and the smouldering peat. I may not like the man, but it's worth visiting to sample his collection.

"The perfect blend of smoke and salt," I comment, taking a sip and savouring the mouthful. "Those Scots knew how to make a drink."

He nods appreciatively and gestures to the chairs by the open fire. "Shall we sit?"

The embers crackle as we get comfortable. He reclines in his chair, studying me. If he wants me to impress him like his other court jesters, I'm the wrong person for the job.

"What can the Dukes do for you, Spencer?" I ask.

"I heard you were the best," Spencer says. "Your reputation precedes you."

"We are," I reply. "But we're selective about our clients. Not everyone can pay our prices."

"Money is no object," Spencer says smugly. "Although you can probably tell that."

I say nothing, waiting for him to get to the point. Clients like Spencer are used to being made to feel like the most special person in the world. They've become accustomed to it and expect it like it's a God-given right, but I'm not here to play games. I check my watch pointedly. He notices, and his lip curls. My time is precious.

"Someone found one of my men, Anthony Steel, dead this morning," Spencer says. "Murdered."

"I'm sure he had many enemies in his line of work," I reply. People are killed all the time, especially in the arms industry. He's likely to have pissed off the wrong person and paid for it. "Why do you need us?"

"This is different." Spencer gulps his drink and winces, but not from the alcohol burn. "He was…"

"He was what?"

"It's better if I show you."

Spencer hands his phone to me, avoiding looking at the screen as his skin drains of colour.

I zoom in to decipher what I'm looking at. Body parts are laid out like pieces of a jigsaw. Anthony's eyes have been scooped out of their sockets, and stab wounds are visible on parts of the skin. What's most disturbing is how his genitals are decimated. They'd be unrecognisable if they weren't positioned between the meaty chunks of what remains of his thighs.

"We found him in his flat," Spencer continues. "He's never been late in the ten years he's worked for me, and he didn't show up this morning."

"It's certainly something," I reply.

The killer has staged his body on the bed, but the cream carpet is clean. There's no blood. Not even a single droplet. He didn't die there. But why risk being seen to take him back to his home? It'd have been easier to dispose of the parts.

Spencer snatches his phone back. "Do you see why I called you now?"

"You have the resources, money, and security," I say. "Why do you need us?"

"My team can deal with score settlers," Spencer says. "But anyone who holds grudges against us wouldn't do it like this. They'd shoot him in the head and claim responsibility. This is…"

"Personal," I finish his sentence.

"Whoever killed Steel hacked into his security system. They got in and out of the flat multiple times without being detected," he says, running a troubled hand through his hair. "It's baffled my security."

"We're not the police," I remind him.

In my twenties, I worked as an officer. I climbed the ranks quickly but became disillusioned by too much politics and not enough action. After that, I started my own business selling weapons overseas. I built good connections and was good at what I did, but it cost me everything. When I returned to the UK after *the incident*, I wanted to leave that life behind. I met a woman who I thought could help me, but I failed her, just like I failed all of them.

"I need your protection," Spencer says. The fire illuminates his fearful eyes. "If they got to Steel, I could be next."

"We can protect you," I say, "but it'll cost you. We require a deposit. Half a million."

It's more than our usual charge, but he can pay it. After all, he's the one who has a bottomless pit of cash to burn.

"Do you accept gold?" He saunters to a bookcase and flips a few books to reveal a hidden safe. With four clicks of a combination lock, it opens. He gets a heavy gold bar and brings it to me to inspect. "You can have this, and I'll transfer the rest."

I turn it in my hands. "That should do it. Now, let me explain how this is going to work." I take a burner phone from my coat pocket and pass it to him. "This is the only phone you can contact us on. We'll give you a new one every week. Our contact number is pre-programmed. First, I need you to send us all the information you have on Steel's death."

"But what about—"

All the bastard cares about is saving his skin.

"Someone will watch you around the clock," I interrupt him. His shoulders relax. "I will report our findings weekly and inform you about any immediate developments. Understood?"

His macho bravado slips for a second, and he murmurs, "Yes."

"Keep the phone on you at all times so we can track your movements," I continue. "We'll send a text later with the rest of the information and a contract for you to sign from a security firm called Royal Protection. Everything will look above board. We will require access to everything—the names of contacts you're meeting, when, and any security systems you have in place. You can't hide anything from us."

Spencer squirms. "Is that really necessary?"

"Absolutely," I reply. "If you wanted to hire human guard dogs, you've come to the wrong people. We're not reactive. We hunt down threats and eliminate them. That's what you're paying us for and what makes the Dukes special."

"Fine," he says flippantly with the arrogance of a man who gets everything he wants. "I get it, okay? I'll follow your rules."

"You'll pay us weekly," I say, wrapping up the deal. "No payment means no protection. Do you agree to those terms?"

Spencer nods.

"And there's one more thing," I say. "You will tell everyone you have employed Royal Protection, but no one can know that we are the Dukes. You can't reveal my identity or my co-workers' identity to anyone. Because if you do, we'll leave you in an even worse position than Steel. Only no one will ever find the pieces."

Spencer gulps. "Understood."

"So we agree, then." I smile and stand, holding my hand out for Spencer to shake. He takes it. His palms are cold and sweaty like a slippery eel when his fingers clasp mine. "It's a pleasure doing business with you."

He calls for his housekeeper to escort me out. When I leave, I look back at the house. The curtains twitch in the first-floor window, then close abruptly again. Strange, but not as strange as the image Spencer showed me. It's rare to see violence that exceeds Callen's brutality levels.

"Well?" Seb asks as I return to the car. "What did he want?"

"I'll explain when we get back to base with the others," I say, trying to shake the image of Steel from my mind.

What kind of monster can do that? When we work out their motive, everything else will fall into place…

CHAPTER 20

CALLEN

"'ll go and speak to her," I tell Bram. He gives me a look that says *it's not like I can*. Sarcastic bastard. "When I've scared him off, you can follow him and find out where he's going."

He nods reluctantly in agreement. He prefers being behind a computer screen, but the fresh air will do him good.

We park and head into the pub to pursue Rose. We're hit with a wall of warmth and the smell of beer. It's busy. Most of the tables are full, and all the groups are standing around talking, but it's easy to spot her red hair. My cock stirs as I picture her lips parting as she moans over Seb's fingers. I didn't lie when I said she looks beautiful when she comes. She's a stick of dynamite, and Seb's selfish to want to keep her to himself.

She and the man are chatting at a table. Bram enters through another entrance, getting into position and watching on from a safe distance.

I saunter past where they are sitting, then stop. "It's Rose, isn't it?" Her blue eyes widen in surprise as she looks up, and then they narrow. "Remember me? I'm Callen, Seb's housemate."

"Yeah, I remember," she says, instantly getting defensive. Does she realise that's a turn-on? I pull out a chair without an invitation and take a seat, making her scowl. "I didn't ask you to join us, arsehole."

"I'm glad we've run into each other again," I say, ignoring her. "I want to apologise for the other night. Why don't I get you a drink to make up for it? Unless I'm interrupting something. Who's your friend?"

The poor shmuck glares at me, annoyed I'm ruining his chances of getting laid.

"Not that it's any of your business, but this is Jake," she snaps. She crosses her arms, drawing attention to those beautiful tits I want to bury my face in. "He's a source for an article I'm writing. We're in the middle of a meeting."

"You're a journalist," I say, pretending he doesn't exist. "I've never been good at writing myself. What's the article about?"

"Torture techniques used in the Vietnamese war," Jake cuts in coldly. "I'm studying for a PhD."

He's not fooling me. This fucker doesn't study history. He has first-hand experience.

"Fascinating," I say, rubbing my chin. Maybe he'll inspire me. Although I doubt he'll teach me anything I don't already know. "Mind if I listen in?"

"Actually, we were just finishing up," Jake—if that's his real name—says. "Do you have all you need, Rose?"

"Uh-huh," she says, flicking through the notes on her phone. "I only needed a few quotes to finish it. Thanks for meeting me at the last minute. You've helped me get out of a bind."

"Where's the article being published?" I press.

"An online history blog," Jake answers.

She's had a narrow escape. How would she feel if she knew she'd interviewed a serial killer? An article about his actual history would gain more readers than whatever drivel she publishes.

"Is there an actual interest in that kind of stuff?" I ask, holding his gaze to let him know I see through him. Yep, it's him, alright—the driver of the car. I reach for the open packet of salt and vinegar crisps on the table. "Cheers, I'm starving."

"Thanks for coming, Jake," Rose says. "I'll send you a draft before it goes live."

"Perfect," Jake replies, standing up. "I look forward to reviewing it."

She shoots him an apologetic smile. "I'm sorry for the interruption."

He hesitates. "Will you be okay?"

"She'll be fine," I snarl. *Back off, motherfucker.* "Have a good night, *Jake.*"

My eyes follow him as he leaves. Yeah, that's right. Keep walking. Bram is waiting at the exit and slips out after him. Now I have her undivided attention.

"Is interrupting people a habit of yours?" Rose says, rising from the table, not waiting for an answer. "I have to go home and type up my notes."

"I'll walk you back," I offer. "London's not a safe place to walk alone at night."

"I'm all set." Rose pulls a rape whistle out of her bag. "See?"

"With an arse like yours, a whistle isn't going to help," I say. Her cheeks flush. "Come on, what kind of friend am I if I let Seb's girlfriend walk home alone, huh?"

"I'm not his girlfriend."

"Still," I say. I tip the crumbs from the crisp packet down my throat. "I may not be an Englishman, but that doesn't mean I'm not a gentleman."

She scoffs. "Someone like you will never be a gentleman."

"So we got off on the wrong foot," I say. "I get that. But there's no harm in me walking you home."

"Fine," she agrees reluctantly. Maybe she senses she's fighting a losing battle. "But I don't want to talk."

She puts on her jacket and marches away, except I'm quicker. I get to the door first and hold it open for her. "After you."

"Don't think this gives the illusion of you having manners," she rebuffs, storming past. "I know exactly what kind of a man you are."

Damn, her smart mouth is sexy.

"What happened to not talking to me?" I ask, hurrying after her. "Or can't you resist?"

"Fuck you." She quickens her pace. I keep up easily, and she sighs in exasperation. "You walking me home is truly unnecessary. I only live a few streets away."

"If something happened to you, what would your boyfriend say?" I ask.

"Didn't you hear me the first time?" She stops and plants her hands on her hips. "Seb is not my boyfriend."

Yeah, I heard her the first and second time. Although I want to hear her say it again… and see how much of a frenzy I can whip her into.

"So you keep saying, princess," I say, closing the gap between us. My gaze lingers on her lips, and she swallows. I'm a good-looking man. She won't be able to hold back much longer. "If he's not your boyfriend, does that mean you'll let anyone finger-fuck you in a club? Is there somewhere I can sign up?"

"You're unbelievable."

Her jaw sets in fury as she struts away. I leave it a few seconds, checking out her arse in those tight jeans from behind, before catching up. It's not difficult when my legs are twice as long as hers.

"Come on," I say. "I'm only playing."

"I don't know why Seb is friends with you," she grumbles.

"Funnily enough, he often asks himself the same question…"

CHAPTER 21
IVY

struggle to see around Callen's broad shoulders. He's got shoulder-length hair, a beard, and an expression that says he doesn't give a shit what anyone thinks of him.

When we take a corner, I glance back at Jonathon on the opposite end of the street. A man follows close behind him. The same man who watched us in the pub. I sensed his presence, and so did Jonathon. We could have handled him together if Callen, the interfering arsehole, didn't interrupt us.

Jonathon's follower is a giant. Six-five, at least. He has cropped black hair with traditional tattoos covering his arms and an outstretched owl inked over his neck. Jonathon will be fine without me. Before we left, his foot nudged mine under the table to tell me he had it covered. Jonathon doesn't need a babysitter... and neither do I.

From my vantage point, I see Jonathon take a purposeful left into an alleyway with a dead end. The man continues in pursuit. It's a shame I can't stay to watch the action. But I've got more pressing issues to contend with, like shaking off my annoying lapdog.

"Do you flirt with every woman you meet?" I ask Callen. "Or only when you're trying to annoy your friend?"

He grins. His gorgeous smile and husky Scottish accent would make most women melt into an incoherent puddle with a single look. It's a pity his personality makes him a total bellend.

"No," he replies. "I'm a man who knows what he wants when he sees it."

His piercing, stormy blue eyes rake over my body, making his intentions clear. I stare back, pleased I'm wearing my contact lenses. After running into Seb unexpectedly, I'm taking no chances. If I'm going to stick around London, I can't blow my cover.

I roll my eyes and break the hypnotic stand-off. "Save it for someone who buys your bullshit."

He's fucking infuriating… and hot. So fucking hot. He's the type of man who'd grab you by the throat, slam you into a wall, and fuck you until you scream his name.

Stop it, Ivy.

Maybe he'd reconsider flirting with me if he discovered what I did last night. I left Steel's limbs for Spencer to find. Hopefully, he liked my belated Christmas gift.

I try to ignore Callen's looming presence as we pass HQ. Stephanie is loading the car outside the house. Where's she going? She doesn't look in our direction as we pass, but she'll be watching. I make an okay signal with my fingers behind my back. I can handle Callen.

"You really can go now," I say as we approach my stooge flat. "I'm almost home and have work to do."

"But it's getting late," Callen says. "And work is boring. Don't you want to let loose and have fun?"

"Fun? With you?" I snort. "I don't think so."

"But you don't know what I'm going to suggest."

"From the look on your face, I don't want to," I reply.

He grabs my arm and forces me to face him. He steps forward, engulfing me in his scent, and bends to whisper, "Sebastian thinks you're a good girl. But I see right through your act, princess."

I freeze. What does he know? I don't move, playing it safe. In my bag, I have a knife disguised as lipstick. I can grab it, and…

"See?" Callen moves closer, so close our bodies almost touch. He reaches out, resting his hand on my hip and scorching me with his fingertips. "I can tell you want me."

I laugh in his face, stepping out of his grasp. Does he think that'll work? His ego's on another level.

"Go to hell, Callen," I bark, whipping him with my hair as I turn and storm away quickly.

"Rose!" He follows. "Wait!"

I've got to give him points for persistence.

"Don't you know when to quit?" I demand.

"I said I'd walk you home," he says. "I'm a man of my word."

"Is that a Scottish saying?"

He laughs. "No, but it's a Callen one."

"Where are you from, anyway?" I ask, wanting to find out more. "How long have you known Seb?"

"Do you want to write a profile on me, princess?" he teases. "I can promise you I'm more interesting than the guy you were speaking to at the pub."

"Can you answer a serious question?" I ask. "Or do you just deflect all the time?"

"I'm from Edinburgh," he says. "And I met Seb through work."

"Work?" His biker vibe and ripped jeans don't scream corporate professionalism. "You're an investor too?"

"I'm into a bit of this and that." He shrugs noncommittally. "Are you surprised?"

"The only thing I'm surprised at is why anyone wants to do business with an arse like you," I reply as we arrive back at the flat. I gesture up at the building. "See? I'm home. You can leave now."

He doesn't listen, staying close behind me as I push open the gate. Now he's really getting on my nerves. Can't he take the hint?

"What the…" My voice trails off as I see the flowers covering the steps. Who cleared out a florist? Piles of roses in varying colours make it impossible for me to pass.

Callen ducks to grab the card from the nearest bouquet, but I snatch it from him before he gets the chance. The note reads:

> *I'm sorry.*
> *Can I get a second chance to make it up*
> *to you?*
> *Dinner. Saturday night. Same place.*
> *I'll be waiting.*
> *Seb.*

I sigh and tuck it into my back pocket. Am I being too harsh? My past makes it hard to trust anyone. He seems like a nice guy… and he's fucking incredible in bed.

I gather the roses into my arms and yelp. "Ouch."

They fall from my grip, and I hold up my index finger. A drop of blood bubbles from the cut. Damn thorns.

"Are you okay?" Callen asks, grabbing my finger to inspect it.

"I'm fine!" I yank it away. "It's just a scratch."

"Let me help you bring them inside," he offers.

"Don't touch anything," I hiss. "I don't need your help."

"What do you think I'm going to do?" Callen raises an eyebrow. "Run away with your bouquet and make a profit selling them? It's Valentine's Day tomorrow, and I'm pretty sure he's cleaned out most of London's supply."

I snicker. The thought is sweet enough, but I don't know what Seb expected me to do with all of them.

"Come on," he pushes, "let me help."

"Only because I don't want to keep listening to you whine," I relent. It'll be quicker than making multiple trips myself. "But you're leaving straight after."

"Now, you're putting words into my mouth, princess…"

I unlock the door, then we collect as many roses as we can.

"Through here," I say, taking a right into the kitchen. The lights come on automatically, detecting our motion. I plop the flowers onto the worktop. "Just put them wherever you find room."

We make sure the space always looks lived in. Unwashed coffee mugs are left on the side, the fridge has food, and my laptop is on the table with fake articles messily strewn around. Little details make a story convincing.

I retrieve a vase from under the sink.

"I don't think that's going to cover it, princess," Callen

comments. He's right. It'll only hold a small bunch. "Seb's a romantic. He loves big gestures. I've not seen him this into someone for a while."

I ignore him, turning on the tap and letting the blasting water drown out his chatter. The flowers can sit in the large basin for now. Stephanie will lose her shit if she finds out about this. She's a sucker for romantic gifts.

"You can go now, Callen," I say, drying my wet hands. "I can deal with the rest of the roses myself."

He doesn't leave. Instead, he runs his hand along the marble worktop and moves towards me. "How's your finger?"

"I told you already, it's nothing," I say, despite the red stains on the tea towel.

I try to hide it, but he notices.

"Let me see," he insists, taking my hand and examining the cut. It's deeper than I thought. His hands are scorching like fire. "You're freezing."

"Bad circulation," I mutter, pulling them away from him.

He takes a seat at the breakfast bar.

"I'd love a brew," he says. *Seriously? Is he joking?* "Three sugars."

CHAPTER 22

BRAM

Great. My inability to speak has lumbered me with surveillance duty. I keep my head down and put my hood up, trying to seal out the drizzle and brisk breeze creeping through the fabric. I deserve a pay rise.

I stay a reasonable distance away from our target, following him through a winding alleyway that grows narrower the deeper we get. I haven't missed this type of work. Give me a system to hack and put me behind a keyboard any day. People are complicated, but code isn't.

Seb will be happy we snatched his girlfriend from the clutches of a suspected killer. I see why he likes her. She's pretty with a face that doesn't attract immediate attention, yet when you notice her, you can't look away. There's something familiar about her, too. Have we met before? No, I think as I shrug it off. Running background checks and staring at a screen most of the day can blur reality sometimes.

The scarred man is talking to someone on the phone.

He doesn't appear suspicious until he takes a second turn. It's a dead-end.

He knows I'm following him.

My hands move to my switchblade, but I won't use it—not unless I have to. Getting out of a violent cycle is why I came to work for Freddie, but I still carry a weapon. Old habits die hard. I've got enough blood on my hands to last a lifetime. The Dukes' primary purpose is to protect. It may lead to murder sometimes, but aiding it differs from taking a person's final breath.

The man stops in his tracks and turns to confront me. "Who are you?"

I don't reply, obviously.

"That's how you want to play it." His expression darkens. "The silent treatment?"

I cock my head to the right, shooting him a questioning stare. He doesn't hesitate. His hands fly to his waistband, and he draws a gun at record speed. I swerve away from the bullet hurtling in my direction. *Motherfucker*. He levels his arm, squeezing the trigger again, but the gun misfires. This is my chance.

I charge forward. I dwarf him in size and hit him at full force. He falls to the ground, and his head slams into the concrete with a thud. I grab his arm, twisting it at the elbow, causing his weapon to slip through his fingers.

He lifts his chin, head-butting me in the jaw. I stagger back, giving him enough space to throw a punch and clamber to his feet. His eyes lock on the gun, but my foot's closer. I kick it, sending it skidding underneath a bin.

He's highly trained, possibly ex-military. His lips pull back, and he comes for me like an animal. I take a clumsy swing, but I'm out of practice. He dodges effortlessly, then retaliates by landing a blow to my cheek. He's stronger than he appears.

"That one's for my car," he sneers. "You're with them, aren't you? The Dukes."

They received our message. This confirms he's one of them. Part of the Killers Club. A club we have to learn more about. I need to take him alive to get answers. My fighting ability is rusty, but what I lack in skill, I make up for in size. I have to use that to my advantage.

I dive at him and tackle him down. My arms squeeze around his torso like a python. He struggles and thrashes to free himself, trying to claw at my eyes. He's playing dirty.

Somewhere amidst the struggle, I grab his hair. It's getting harder to hold him. I need him to stop. In desperation, I slam his head into the ground. He stops moving.

Fuck.

I stand on shaky legs, watching a pool of blood form a halo around his head as it laps at my trainers. This is why I stay out of the field. I have no control over my strength. I never meant to kill him.

I kneel and take his pulse. It's slowing. He won't be alive for long if he keeps losing blood at this rate.

"Hey!" a voice bounces off the buildings. I spin to see an attractive woman with long blonde hair rushing towards us in crazy heels. "What's happening? Is he okay?"

I don't answer. I'm already running past her at full speed, hoping I've not killed our only potential lead.

CHAPTER 23

CALLEN

Annoying her is way too much fun. That's something she and Seb have in common. Rose whirls around. If she was a mythological creature, her red hair would transform into snakes, and her venomous stare would turn me to stone. There's nothing hotter than a woman who wants me but denies it.

"First, you insist on walking me home when I don't want your help," she says, storming to where I'm sitting at the breakfast bar. She jabs her finger into my chest to make her point. It doesn't hurt, though the fact she thinks it does is cute. "Then you invite yourself inside, and now you want a cup of fucking tea?"

I slip off the stool, towering over her. She steps back, leaving a small space between her and the kitchen island. I put my arms on either side of her body, boxing her in. I nod my head at the bag slung over her shoulder. "You could use your whistle."

She uses both hands to push me away. The little firecracker has hidden strength. I like that.

"Go to hell, Callen."

"I think you like me," I purr. Her cheeks flush. Yeah, she fucking likes it—even if she doesn't want to admit it. "Seb's a gentleman. He can take you for dinner at the best restaurants and buy you flowers, but he doesn't make your heart race like I do. You don't look at him like you're looking at me right now. Do you want to know my theory?"

She juts her chin out in defiance. Her tone drips with sarcasm as she says, "I have a feeling you're going to tell me anyway."

"I think you're hiding something. An inner rage you don't let people see," I say, reaching behind me to flick the kettle to boil. I really do want a cup of tea. "I don't know why. Maybe it's because you're a journalist in a cutthroat world. Who am I to say? But I see it behind your eyes. You're fucking furious, aren't you?"

"You know nothing about me," she says through gritted teeth.

"There." I clap my hands. "That's what I'm talking about. There's the rage. You don't show that to Seb, do you?"

Her small hands ball into fists as the kettle hisses. The water bubbles, and steam pours from its spout.

"But you can show me." I twirl a strand of her red hair around my finger. "You don't have to hide anything from me. Underneath your sweet act, you're a fucking lion. And I can see that because you're just like me."

"I swear to God, Callen, I'll—"

I put my finger to her lips. "What're you going to do, princess?" I smirk. "Kill me?"

CHAPTER 24

IVY

Callen's joking, but he doesn't know how close I am to wrapping the kettle cord around his neck to choke him. I've never met anyone who has been able to get under my skin so fast. He's burrowing his way in deep, and I want to tear him out.

I hate him.

I fucking hate him!

"What're you going to do, princess?" he asks in his no-good sexy, husky voice.

My nipples harden from the warmth radiating off him. How is that fair? My body is acting irrationally.

Maybe I should kill him. Slashing his throat would be nice, quick, and painless. Being in the kitchen would make clean-up simple, although he is Seb's friend…

Someone would inevitably ask questions, and Alaric would be furious. I can hear his lecture now: we're not serial killers, we're trained professionals, we don't kill for free, blah, blah, blah. But I want to kill him. I really want to.

Callen edges closer, invading my personal space. There's an inch between us now. My gaze lingers on the stack of kitchen knives and how liberating it would be to drive them into his flesh to stop his mindfuckery.

Callen is right about one thing, however. He's nothing like Seb. Seb *is* a gentleman—granted, one with a penchant for public sex, but he genuinely gives a shit. But Callen? He wants to provoke a reaction. It's how he gets his kicks. The best way to deal with people like him is to use the grey rock method, but he's wound me up so much that I'm blinded to reason.

"You can deny you want me," he says in a low growl. His stare lingers on my pointed nipples as he licks his lips and fucks me with his eyes. "But I can sense it. You want me to bend you over and fuck you right here, don't you?"

I back away. My arse hits the cold marble as his muscular arms at my sides leave me no escape. He presses his body into mine, and I feel the outline of his thick cock against my stomach.

"You bastard," I spit as the kettle howls.

"Maybe I am," he says, running his fingertips playfully along the waistband of my jeans.

His electrifying touch makes my pussy tingle with longing. How is he having this effect on me? I'm supposed to be an unshakable killer. Except Callen sees *me*. He doesn't know who I am or how I like to spend my time, but he sees my rage… and that's both fucking terrifying and freeing.

"I promise you won't regret it," he says. "I can make all those dirty thoughts running through your head a reality, princess."

"Fuck you."

"That's not an answer." He leans to grab a discarded rose and picks off a petal. "Yes?" He plucks another and lets it flutter to the floor. "Or no?"

I capture the fragile flowerhead in my palm, behead the rose, and hurl it across the room. "Does that answer your question?"

"I knew it," he says. "You're not like other women. I want to see that storm raging inside you, princess. I'm your only way to release it."

"I hate you," I snarl.

I really fucking do. My hate consumes me, making my entire body shake. Self-discipline is the only thing standing between my desires and Callen's blood filling the cracks between the kitchen tiles.

His eyes light up; they're an inferno of chaos. They penetrate me and show how much of a twisted fucker he is. Callen's dark side is vicious. I should stay away from him, but I can't look away.

"I know you hate me," he replies as he strokes the skin above the button on my jeans. "And that's why you don't want me to leave."

If I can't kill him, I have to…

A primal instinct takes over and I dive at him like a wildcat. My hands yank his long hair, forcing his face down to mine. When we kiss, it's like a bomb exploding.

He sweeps the crockery and roses off the side with one muscled arm and an almighty crash. My lips don't leave his as he grabs my arse, turns us around, and hoists me onto the island. Petals and smashed ceramics lie destroyed in the wake of the hurricane that forced his way into my house.

"You're paying for the damage," I growl, then sink my

teeth into his lip so hard that it fills my mouth with the coppery metallic taste of his blood.

He pulls back and grins. Blood drips down his chin, and he wipes his mouth with the back of his hand. He's a psycho.

"You're going to like my method of payment, princess," he promises.

He spreads my legs wide, positioning himself between them. We're predators caught in a feeding frenzy. I claw his back, tearing his skin, while he rips the front of my shirt to expose my breasts.

Why didn't I wear a bra today? He squeezes my tits hard, making them bulge, as his mouth finds my nipples. I hate myself for the reluctant moan he draws from my throat when he sucks on them.

I tug at his t-shirt. He pauses for a second, throwing his jacket to the floor and yanking the shirt over his head. My fingers are already scratching at the muscles underneath. He's ripped as fuck with a layer of hair and scars. Lots of scars. Scars I'd love to add to.

He undoes the button and zipper on my jeans. I move my arse so he can yank them off. He goes to kiss me, but I grab his hair, wrapping it around my fist until I'm holding it tight. I force his head back and push him down between my legs, letting him know what I want. He doesn't give in easily. He bites my inner thighs, hard enough that they'll bruise.

I gasp. "I fucking hate you."

"Oh, princess…" Callen laughs as he pulls off my knickers. He admires my glistening pussy and licks his lips. "You're going to hate me even more when I make you come harder than you ever have before. You're going to hate me so much you'll be screaming my name for the whole of London to hear."

I hook my knees over his shoulders, and he pulls me forward, burying his face in my heat. He isn't gentle. He fucking devours me. His beard tickles as his tongue probes and pushes into my wetness.

My thighs quiver as I tighten my grip, squeezing his head between my thighs and locking him there. My eyes flicker closed, and I cry out as I writhe against his face to chase my pleasure. Callen thinks he's the villain, but I'm the real monster.

He battles out of my hold, and I growl in disappointment as he stands.

"Now I understand why Seb's obsessed with you," he says with a mischievous glint in his eyes. His chin shines from my juices and smeared blood. "Your cunt tastes as sweet as your name."

"You—"

He grabs my throat with one hand to silence me while the other slips between my legs. My pussy stretches to fit three of his big fingers. He fucks me in harsh strokes, hard enough to make my tits bounce, and squeezes my throat to hold me in place. He's taking from me, and my body craves it.

"See?" Callen purrs. "You want this as much as I do. Since I saw you come, I've wanted to feel your sweet cunt squeeze my fingers."

Seb is calculated, each touch designed to feel amazing, but Callen is brutal. He doesn't draw or tease out an orgasm like Seb. No, Callen pillages it. My pussy is a village, and he's come with a pitchfork to burn it to the ground, and I've handed him the fucking match.

Usually, I try to free myself from a chokehold, but I

lean into his touch, rocking my hips into him to amplify the toe-curling sensation. He keeps going until I'm panting and right on the edge of exploding when... he stops.

He undoes his belt and drops his trousers with arrogant confidence. His thick cock with a Prince Albert piercing matches his menacing personality.

"I'm not like Seb, princess." Callen spits on his cock and slathers himself with it. "Seb gives you what you want, but I will give you what you need. And right now, your pussy wants to be pounded so hard you won't be able to walk tomorrow."

He pulls me from the island, spins me, and throws me forward to press my tits onto the worktop. He doesn't waste any time. His cock slams into me roughly from behind in a single thrust, and the sound of his giant hand slapping my arse echoes around the kitchen.

"Now I really see why Seb doesn't want to share you," he murmurs gruffly as he pulls my hair into a ponytail and wrenches it, making my scalp sting and my eyes water.

I grit my teeth as my pussy clings to him, getting wetter with each thrust. I hate him more than ever for having this effect on me. All I have to do is grab the corkscrew and plunge it into his neck to put a stop to it, but I don't. The tip of his piercing rubs my G-spot, and I cry out.

"You like this, don't you, princess?" His words sent shivers down my spine. Why is his accent so sexy? "You take my cock so fucking well. Can you take the whole thing?"

Wait, there's more?

"Yes," I moan reluctantly.

My pussy aches, stretching to accommodate him as he thrusts even deeper into me. Pressure builds in my core, and the rhythmic pound of his slamming hips is about to make me come, until…

A noise from outside pulls me from the moment.

"Wait," I say as Callen's cock rails so deep into me that his soft hair brushes my arse cheeks. He doesn't move, staying frozen inside me, and I'm on high alert as I whisper, "Do you hear that?"

CHAPTER 25

SEB

Where the hell are they? Ten calls have gone straight to their voicemails, and I tracked their car, which hasn't moved from the same spot. They should have been back by now.

"I'm going to meet the others at the pub," I say to Freddie, casually slinging my jacket over my shoulder. "We have to make the most of our freedom before starting the new job tomorrow."

I don't bother asking him to join us because I already know the answer. I stopped inviting him years ago. Sometimes I miss my old friend, but tonight, I'm happy about his anti-social tendencies.

Freddie used to enjoy partying. Now, work consumes every second of his day. It's an obsession. The Dukes are everyone's top priority, but they're Freddie's entire identity. His hard work has paid off, but it's dominated his life. We've expanded to add Bram and Callen to our ranks, invested in the right places, and grown a stellar reputation despite the recent mishap, but it's never enough for him.

As I leave, Freddie doesn't look up from his computer

screen. He's busy scrolling through the files Spencer Bexley—our newest client—sent. After examining a photograph of skewered testicles, I could do with a strong drink.

When I'm outside, I ring the others again. Nothing. *Motherfuckers.* There's no point involving Freddie until I have more information. He'll be annoyed I didn't mention their sighting of the scarred man, but misidentifications always happen. For all I know, Bram and Callen are having a piss-up. It's my situation to handle. I'm the Dukes' second in command. If something's gone wrong, I need to fix it before involving the boss.

I drive the Maserati towards the pub where Rose was last seen. I'll pass her flat en route. My jaw clenches as I drive by her building. I have a split-second decision to make: go to the pub or check on her first. My hands know what I want before my mind does as I swerve. There's no choice. Unlike the Dukes, Rose is defenceless. I'll focus better if I know she's safe.

Before banging down her door like a crazy stalker, I try calling her. *This is Rose. I can't come to the phone right now.* I huff in frustration at the pre-recorded message. Why have a phone if you don't answer it? Fuck it. I unbuckle my seat belt and pace up her steps. A single rose lies discarded on the doorstep.

I pick it up and ring the doorbell, then… A crash from inside makes me spring into action.

"Rose," I yell, pounding on the door with my fist. I'll break it down if I have to. "Let me in!"

I press my ear against it and crane my neck to see through her window. Shadows of people move behind the drawn blinds. I take a step back, ready to charge, when the door flies open.

I sigh in relief at seeing her. "Rose."

My eyes trail down her body, taking in her thin t-shirt and hard nipples under the fabric. She tugs the hem down to try to cover her bare legs beneath.

"What are you doing here, Seb?" she asks breathlessly. Her cheeks are rosy, like she's been working out. "Are you trying to wake the entire street?"

Shit. I need an excuse to be here that doesn't involve her having a drink with a potential serial killer.

Holding the rose in my hand, I stammer, "I wanted to see whether you got my flowers."

A deep Scottish rumble responds from inside, "Oh, she got them…"

I glimpse over her shoulder at the figure stepping out of a room with a tartan tea towel wrapped around his waist. Her smudged lipstick, her out-of-place hair, her flushed chest. No…

"Seb, I—" Rose begins.

She can't meet my gaze, confirming my suspicions. I set my sights on Callen and see red. I push Rose out of the way. I want blood. His blood.

"I'll kill you!" I roar.

"Seb, don't," Rose shouts from behind me, but she can't hold me back.

I grab Callen and pin him to the wall, wedging my arm under his chin.

"You asked me to look after her," Callen replies with a smug smirk. "That's exactly what I did."

I cut off his airways, wanting to watch his life drain away. This is a game to him. He knows how much I like her, and he's using her to get to me for his own twisted amusement.

"Seb!" Rose's piercing tone cuts through my anger. She claws at my shoulders. "Stop it!"

I look to the kitchen on my right. Petals and broken kitchenware litter the floor like there's been a struggle. My anger dissipates, and fear lodges itself in my throat.

"Did he hurt you?" I ask.

"No," she replies, still clutching my single pathetic rose and hanging her head. "I don't know what came over me."

I let Callen go. He slumps down the wall, clutching his throat and gasping for air. He's lucky to still be breathing.

"She wanted it, Seb," Callen croaks tauntingly. Still, he doesn't quit. "Her tight little pussy was so wet for me."

I punch him in the stomach to shut him up. I don't want to hear it.

Why him? Anyone else would be better. He's a crazed psychopath who brings trouble wherever he goes.

"I can see why you like her," Callen splutters. "Such a sweet-tasting cunt." He winks. "And she likes it rough."

"Don't talk about her like that," I warn, pulling my fist back.

"That's enough." Rose catches my wrist before I break his nose. "Let him go."

I reluctantly drop my arm, using every ounce of my self-control. My breathing is ragged as the bitter notes of betrayal ripple through me.

"She loved every fucking second," Callen says, taking advantage of my hesitation.

Rose narrows her eyes and shoots a glare of sheer hatred in his direction.

"Shut the fuck up, Callen," she hisses, "or I'll punch you myself."

"Go for it, princess," Callen says, still wheezing but lavishing in the chaos.

"Why him?" I murmur.

"I..." She can't justify herself and won't look me in the eye. "I... it just...."

"Don't lie and say it just happened," Callen interrupts. The bastard is pushing her buttons, goading her, wanting to tip her over the edge. "You wanted me from the minute you saw me. If you deny it, you're only lying to yourself."

Rose slaps him hard. His head jerks to the right with a satisfying sound. Despite my fury, I grin at how she isn't afraid to take on a man twice her size.

Callen rubs the red handprint on his cheek. "Ouch."

"I meant it when I said I hate you," she sneers.

Suddenly, everything clicks into place. Now I see how it happened. Supercharged energy buzzes between them. I've never seen this side of Rose before, and damn... I wish I hated it. It'd be easier that way, but I don't. It only makes me like her more. She's fierce and stares into the eyes of a monster without backing down. She's not afraid of him, and that's why Callen likes her. There's a fine line between lust and hate.

"She's feisty," Callen remarks, licking his lips. "You know how much I like that." He turns to me and grins. "Are you done playing the jealous boyfriend act? You can give Rose what she was craving before your rude interruption, or you can leave us to pick up where we left off. The choice is yours."

Rose isn't my girlfriend. I have no right to be mad at her, but Callen? He's damaged and dangerous. I'm not leaving her alone with him. Over my dead fucking body.

"What are you talking about?" Rose asks.

"Do you know what's better than being fucked by one man?" He strokes her cheek. She catches his wrist and wrenches it away like she wants to tear his fingers off. I wish I could do it for her. "Being fucked by two men at once."

"You're irreprehensible," she hisses, but her pupils dilate.

Does she want this?

The two of us at the same time?

"Isn't that part of the fun?" Callen teases. "Don't lie to me. I can smell how wet you are from here."

"Callen," I warn. "Enough."

"But this is what she wants, Seb," he continues. "Your perfect little Rose isn't such a good girl, after all. She wants to be fucked like a dirty whore. Why don't you bend over and show Seb the bruises on your arse from how hard I spanked you, princess?"

My anger rises again, and I charge, knocking him to the floor. I climb on top of him, pinning him down with my thighs. *Thwack!* I land a punch to his jaw, and he laughs hysterically.

"He didn't hurt me," Rose shrieks. She climbs onto my back like a spider monkey, but her strength doesn't match mine. I keep punching, splitting his cheek open. "Seb, I wanted it, okay?"

I freeze. Her words pierce my heart like a blade twisting in my chest. I stand and straighten my suit jacket, now flecked with Callen's blood. The fight inside me extinguishes.

"Do you want me to go?" I ask.

By go, I mean, wait until Callen departs, then beat the shit out of him.

"No." She grabs my hand to tug me towards her. "Don't."

"Why him?" I nudge my head to Callen, who is recovering his junk with the tea towel. My irritation bubbles to the surface. "Why do you want me when you have him? Can't he give you everything you need?"

"I know you're mad, but I've done nothing wrong." Her voice is soothing and rational. "You're not my boyfriend, and I told you that I don't date, but..."

Sure, we've only been on one date, and I have no right to be this furious, but I can't help myself. Since we met, she's all I've thought about, and I don't want him to have her. He can't.

"But what?" I snap.

"I like you," she mumbles.

"And I really fucking like you, if you haven't noticed," I say. "But this?" I shake my head at Callen's naked arse heading into her living room. "I don't know if I can do this."

I'm not talking about tonight. I'm talking about every-thing. Me. Her. *Us.* If there even is an us. She senses it too.

"I want you to stay." Her fingers stroke mine. Her gaze is pleading as she whispers, "Isn't that enough for now?"

Is it? Staying means being okay with the fact she's fucked a guy who she thinks is my friend. This means being fine with how she might suddenly stop talking to me. This means accepting she might walk out of my life one day and I'll never see her again.

"Do you feel the same way about me and him?" I ask, unable to keep my insecurity from creeping into my tone.

"No," Rose says vehemently. "I hate him, but..."

"You want him," I finish her sentence. "Don't you?"

She bites her lip, battling with her conflicting thoughts. Admitting she wants him seems to pain her more than their being together bothered me.

"Rose?" I prompt. "You can say it."

"I... want him, okay?" Her body language changes

when she talks about him, as if a dark side of her psyche is being summoned to the surface. Callen has a natural gift for bringing out the worst in people. Her voice softens again. "But that doesn't change anything between us."

An emotion stirs behind her eyes. A single look that gives me a glimmer of hope that we could be something more—even if she doesn't know it yet.

CHAPTER 26

IVY

Seb's shoulders slump, but he doesn't move. Fuck. I've hurt him. Seeing the hurt in his eyes stings more than a DIY Hollywood wax. Why do I care about his feelings? I shouldn't. He knows I don't do relationships. Getting attached to someone is too dangerous, but…

I step closer, craving his warmth. Needing it. Needing his touch. "I never meant to hurt you, Seb."

I don't blame him for being mad. He sent me the biggest bunches of roses I've ever seen. Then I fucked his friend.

Who does that?

Someone Seb should stay away from, but he's still here.

I rise on my tiptoes and brush my lips against his. I expect him to push me away—it's what I deserve—only he doesn't.

"Do you really want this?" he murmurs, wrapping his arms around my waist. "You want us both?"

I find myself nodding. Callen lives and breathes destruction. As much as I want to kill him, he drives me wild. Callen whips me into an untamed frenzy, caught in a carnal battle for dominance. Seb is the opposite. I'm drawn to him like a magnet. He's a steadying force, an anchor. I can't deny my attraction to them both.

Seb's tongue plunders my mouth. It's filled with passion and something else too. Possessiveness.

"You don't know what you're getting yourself into," Seb warns, pulling away and resting his nose on mine. His erection rubs against me. "Callen's a monster."

"I thought I heard my name," Callen says, standing in the living room doorway. I turn as he drops the tea towel to reveal his raging boner. "Have you kissed and made up already?"

"I swear to God, Callen," Seb growls, "if you hurt a single hair on her head, I'll kill you."

"I won't hurt her," Callen purrs. He creeps behind me, resting his cock between my arse cheeks. I had no time to put my knickers back on before Seb's surprise appearance. My eyes stay fixed on Seb's as Callen brushes a strand of hair off my neck and licks along my skin, then adds, "Not unless she wants me to."

I observe Seb's reaction, expecting him to throw another punch. I'm a wall between them, a barrier, but he doesn't make a move—despite his clenched jaw telling me he wants to.

I wrap my arms around Seb's neck to pull him closer. His tense shoulders relax a bit as I cautiously slide off his jacket and let it drop to the floor at our feet. In response, he cups my face in his giant hands and kisses me. My lips part as I reach for his buttons. It's an expensive shirt, so I carefully undo them one by one, then help him shrug it off. He's gorgeous. My fingers dance across his chest, running along the deep, etched outlines of his muscles.

Meanwhile, Callen's cock nudges me like the devil's hot poker, demanding my attention. His hand slides between my legs from beneath to find my hot heat. He slides two fingers along my pussy, teasing my entrance before pushing them inside me. I moan into Seb's mouth as Callen's fingers curl and stroke my G-spot.

Seb breaks our kiss and grabs the hem of my shirt. He pulls it over my head, giving him a perfect view of Callen's hand buried inside me right down to the knuckles. I freeze. Will he leave? Instead, he licks his finger, coating it with spit.

I search Seb's gaze and ask, "Are you sure about this?"

He doesn't reply but answers my question by circling my engorged clit that's begging to be touched. My toes curl. It's a struggle to stay standing, but being wedged between them keeps me upright.

Callen's breath on my neck sends shivers down my spine. "This is what you need, princess."

Seb's fingers slide down to meet Callen's. I moan as he parts my pussy lips to squeeze another inside me. Having both of them inside me turns me on even more. They move together in a rhythm, creating a build-up of tingling pressure.

"Fuck," I gasp, feverishly stroking Seb's bulge over his trousers as my orgasm nears.

Fury and lust ignite in his eyes as he takes his finger out of me with a pop and licks it clean.

"Where's your bedroom?" Seb growls.

"Upstairs," I reply. "First door on the left."

"Why go to the bedroom?" Callen questions with a mischievous smirk. "We can have her right here in the hallway."

Callen spins me to face him and grabs my throat. He

turns, pushes me into the wall with a bang, parts my legs roughly, and drops to his knees. Under normal circumstances, I'd knock his teeth out, but I push my pussy into his face instead. I prop my foot up on his shoulder to give him a better angle, and then he eats me out like a pussy-munching demon.

Seb watches on, and I bite my bottom lip, trying to contain my moans. Until, suddenly, Callen stops. I huff in irritation as he runs a finger down my slit. I'm done with his teasing.

He turns to Seb. "Do you want to try her?" The bastard is treating me like his dessert. "She tastes so fucking good."

Seb's cock twitches in response.

"Move," Seb grunts.

Callen moves out of the way. I slide my hand into Seb's trousers, then tug them down. Seb's firm hands grasp my arse and hoist me into the air. He won't torture me like Callen. I wrap my legs around his inked torso, clinging on tightly as he slides himself over my wetness.

"Please," I whimper as his tip rubs teasingly against my dripping entrance. "I want you."

He doesn't make me beg. He gives me exactly what I want. He penetrates me and bounces my body up and down his shaft like I'm weightless.

"Fuck, Seb," I groan, clinging to his neck and breathing in his scent. "Yes."

Callen's on his feet again. He stares at my tits and smirks.

"That's right, Seb," Callen encourages. "Fuck her like the dirty whore she is."

Seb quickens his pace, slamming into my pussy harder.

"Hold on," he grunts.

He manages to stay inside me as he carries me through to the living room and lays me on the sofa. Now he lets loose. His thrusts get harder and deeper as the force of him on top of me pushes me into the soft cushions.

Callen follows, watching over Seb's shoulders, and starts touching himself. He catches my eye and winks. Watching him pleasure himself is fucking hot. All I can hear is the wet slap of Seb's balls against me. My pussy clings to him, about to come, when he pulls out, leaving me panting and confused. If I don't come soon, someone is going to die!

"Is this your way of punishing me?" I demand as he stands next to Callen.

They look down at me, and I sit up, resisting the urge to give myself the release I desperately crave.

"Don't you remember what I said, princess?" Callen says. His cock is right in my face, and he slaps my cheek with it. "We'll give you what you need, not what you want."

Fuck that. I grab his cock with my fist and squeeze, making it turn purple. Maybe his piercing will pop out if I squeeze hard enough.

"What I need is for you to shut the fuck up," I retort.

Seb sits at my side and grabs my chin, turning my attention from Callen. He orders, "Ride me, Rose."

With Callen's cock still in my hand, I mount Seb, facing away from him. He's big, but I sink down easily, drenching him.

"Fuck," Callen groans as a bead of pre-cum pools from his bulging dick. "Let me see if your mouth feels as good as your cunt."

He grabs my hair in a rough ponytail to guide my mouth to his cock. I take him as Seb's fingers find my clit.

Fuck. Callen forces his way down my throat, hitting my tonsils and making me gag.

"Don't hurt her," Seb warns.

"She's not a China doll," Callen growls, pushing his dick deeper and silencing me with it. "This is what she needs. Look at her spit dripping all over my balls. She wants this as much as we do."

Callen's right.

My pussy clings to Seb's cock as I choke on Callen's. My chest heaves as Seb works my clit to the point of aching. The slightest touch is going to make me...

Shit.

I can't hold it anymore...

I come undone and scream onto Callen's cock. The vibrations must move through his body as, seconds later, he blasts his load, giving me no choice but to swallow it. My pussy drowns Seb, and I come harder than I ever have in my life. Seb's hips jerk underneath me. I rock, drawing every drop of pleasure out, until he grunts and fills me with his cream.

What the fuck just happened?

While I'm still reeling, Callen extracts himself and wipes a glob of his cum off my chin with his thumb and pops it in his mouth. He grins at Seb and says, "I don't know about you, but I could get used to this."

The front door rattles and makes me jump. I stumble off Seb's cock in a daze.

"Bethany?" I call, trying to alert Stephanie to the fact that other people are here. I grab a nearby blanket to cover myself, then hobble to see her standing at the end of the hallway.

"I see you've been busy," she says, raising her eyebrows at the mess in the kitchen and the heap of discarded clothes. "Have you forgotten about our early flight?"

A flight? Something's happened. Something bad. She's been telling me to get laid for years. She wouldn't interrupt unless shit hit the fan.

"I'll be upstairs packing," she says.

That's code for *get everyone out of the house, because we need to talk...*

CHAPTER 27

SEB

Rose talks to Bethany, her flatmate—I recognise her voice from the bar. Their conversation floats down the hallway, so I can't help overhearing. Why didn't she mention she's flying somewhere tomorrow? Footsteps pad upstairs, fading into the distance as Rose returns.

"You guys need to leave," she says, clutching the blanket to her chest to stop it from unravelling. Her tone is matter-of-fact, business-like almost. The rosy glow to her cheeks has dulled. "Like, right now."

"Where are you flying to?" I ask, unable to contain my curiosity.

"It's a last-minute research trip." She shrugs dismissively. "We're rolling it into a girl's weekend. Bethany could do with cheering up."

Callen smirks. "We'll leave you to it, princess."

His cock swings like a pendulum as he saunters over to kiss her.

"Don't even think about it." She swerves his attempt

and glowers at him. She may have wanted to fuck him, but he's no competition. "Get the fuck out, Callen."

He cackles and disappears around the corner to retrieve his clothes, leaving an awkward silence stretching between us. There are no rules for this kind of thing. What're you supposed to say to the girl you like when you've watched her swallow the cum of a serial killer?

Callen had a lucky escape. When I first saw them together, I wanted to choke him to death but sharing her changed that. My jealousy hasn't completely vanished, although her pleasure has become my driving force. My determination to make her pussy gush overrode any murderous thoughts about sharing her.

I stand and walk past her, deciding it's better to say nothing than risk offending her again.

"Wait." Rose catches my arm. "How about another date when I get back? Without Callen."

I arch an eyebrow. "But you don't date."

She made that perfectly clear.

"I don't," she admits. A mischievous smile crosses her face that makes her freckles dance and my stomach flutter. "Then again, I guess I can make an exception."

I stroke her cheekbone, trailing my fingers over her smooth skin. "So, you want to see me again?"

Her lips barely move as she whispers, "Yes."

"And what happened with Callen…"

"That's just sex," she says firmly. Do I mean more to her than that? "Nothing more."

"Do you want that to happen again, too? With him?"

"I don't know." She sighs, unable to meet my probing gaze. I've asked the wrong question, and she's pulling away. Whenever we seem to make progress, she shuts me out, like she's terrified of getting too close to me. "I don't know if I can give you what you want. If you want a girl-friend to take to dinner every night, that's not me. My work schedule is crazy, and I—"

A sinking feeling replaces the floaty sensation in my chest. She's backtracking and trying to justify not seeing me again. I won't let that happen. Before she makes more excuses, I interrupt her and finish her sentence, "Like fucking two guys at once?"

I'm only joking to lighten the mood, but it only makes her gasp. I put my hands on her hips and tug her closer.

"Rose, I'm not saying I want to marry you, but I like you. I don't want to see anyone else. I understand you can't make that commitment to me, but I want to make a deal."

She narrows her eyes suspiciously. "I'm listening."

"I know you're independent. You're not my property. You don't belong to me or anyone else," I say. "However, if you're going to fuck other people, I want to be there."

She scans my face to check whether I'm joking and blinks hard when she realises I mean it. "You're serious, aren't you?"

"Deadly."

Rose is a beacon for dangerous men. First me, then the man from the Killers Club, and now, Callen. She's oblivious to how she's been surrounded by murderers. She's vulnerable, and I must protect her.

"I don't sleep around," she says. "Granted, it may not seem like it. It's been years, and now you and Callen are the only men I've slept with. I don't plan on sleeping with the whole of London."

"Even if you do, it won't change my mind," I say,

daring to voice my feelings. "I'm only interested in you. I won't hold you back, tie you down, or ask for any more commitment, but that's the only thing I ask for in return. If you fuck anyone else, I have to be there."

She chews her lip, then blows a loose strand of hair out of her face in exasperation. "Okay, but I don't think it's going to—"

"Shh." I put a finger to her lips. She agreed. That's all I needed to hear. "You better pack for your flight."

I tenderly kiss her forehead, then start getting dressed as she stays in the same spot, still dazed. Callen's nowhere to be seen. The fucker has gotten what he wants, so he's already let himself out.

Rose pokes her head around the living room door to watch me leave.

"Text me when you land," I say. "I'll see you on that date when you get back, and make sure you lock the door behind me."

She rolls her eyes. "Don't worry, I'll make sure no crazy killers can come in."

I bite my tongue to stop myself from adding that it's not stopped us before.

Out on the street, Callen leans against Rose's gate. He winks as soon as he sees me. "Good night, huh?"

I scowl and bash into his shoulder as I pass. "Shut up."

He trots along behind me like a puppy. Emptying his balls has given him renewed energy. "Can I hitch a ride?"

"Only if you don't say another word about what happened tonight."

"Why not?" he jokes. "Are you sure you don't want to compare performance notes?"

"That's it," I declare as we reach my car. "I'm done."

I get into the driver's side and lock all the other doors.

"Hey!" Callen pounds on the window and tries the handle. "What did I say? Open the door!"

That motherfucker is walking home.

CHAPTER 28
IVY

"Don't go there," I warn as Stephanie's questioning gaze burns into me like a laser beam. "No questions."

We pace through the streets back to HQ. The chill bites my fingers as I drag along a suitcase on the off-chance Seb or Callen drive by. Protecting my cover is a pain in the arse. Before leaving, I asked Penelope to book me a fake flight to Dublin and hack into airport security to feign a check-in. She'll keep me posted on the flight path to make my story believable. Details matter. Mistakes happen when you get sloppy. She'd usually alter the airport security camera footage too, except a member of the public won't be able to grant us access to those, so it saves her a job.

"Come on, you can't expect me to say nothing," Stephanie says. "You've gone from years of celibacy to fucking two guys at once. What happened?"

I'm still trying to figure that out myself. Did having sex with Seb unleash five years of horniness? As soon as I spread my legs once, the floodgates opened—literally.

Maybe Seb's dick has the magical ability to separate my pussy from my brain. Earth-shattering orgasms must affect your judgement in some way, right?

"My sex life is none of your business." The fact I have a sex life at all is crazy. I change the subject. "Are you going to tell me why we're rushing to HQ?"

"You know I'd never disturb a cockfest if it wasn't serious." The corners of her lips twitch, and then a brick wall crashes over her features. Her eyes darken. I'm speaking to Stephanie, the killer, now. Her playfulness is gone as she reports, "It's Jonathon. He's hurt."

"How badly?" I ask with no emotion.

Getting hurt is unusual when you're trained by the best in the business, but it happens. Maybe Jonathon got cocky and made a mistake.

"Bad enough to slip into a coma," she replies matter-of-factly as we climb the steps to HQ.

"Well, shit..."

"He'll be okay," Stephanie says dismissively, as if he's grazed his knee. We've all lived through worse. Her heels clip-clop through the foyer to the elevator. "The doc wants to reduce the swelling in his brain. He hit his head pretty hard. Well, someone hit it for him."

My mind backtracks, rewinding to the start of the night at the bar and playing it like a film on fast-forward. I know who did this. I picture his face now—the face of the man who slipped out after Jonathon.

"A guy was watching us at the bar," I say. My brow crinkles as I try to remember. "He's built like a fucking house. He has dark, cropped hair and a tattoo of—"

"An owl on his neck?" Stephanie offers. Her eyes narrow into murderous slits. "Yeah, I saw him flee the scene. The motherfucker ran straight past me. If there wasn't a crowd of people nearby, I'd have made the shot."

We arrive at the medical room to find Jonathon out cold on the bed, surrounded by the whirr of beeping machines. Wires and tubes hang from his arms, and a blood-soaked bandage is wrapped around his head. When he wakes, I'll make a Mr Bump joke.

"I should have followed him." My anger rises, not only at Jonathon's attack but at myself. "I should have—"

"You followed protocol," Alaric finishes my sentence. He approaches from behind us. "You kept your cover."

"Yeah, she kept her cover alright," Stephanie mumbles.

I elbow her in the ribs to shut her up. Even though she and Alaric share most things, I don't need him to know how I spent my evening. The irony isn't lost on me that while Jonathon's head was getting pounded into the ground; I was busy being pounded by a thick…

"Is he a Duke?" I ask, pushing aside the ache between my legs. "The guy who attacked him?"

"We can't be sure," Alaric says. "But we think so."

"Are we hunting him down already?" I ask. "Has Penelope found him?"

With facial recognition and the number of cameras in London, she can find anyone with a few clicks. After a few more, she can pull an entire file documenting your whole life. No one can hide from us.

"We don't need Penelope to make an ID," Alaric says with a clenched jaw. "I already know who he is from Stephanie's description. His name is Bram Deveraux. We have history."

"History?" My ears perk up. Most people don't get the chance to have a history with Alaric. Everyone who crosses him dies. "What kind of history?"

Alaric glances at Stephanie. The way she squirms makes me stand straighter. This must be juicy.

"What is it?" I demand. "I can tell when you're hiding something."

"He used to work for Bexley," Stephanie says, choosing her words carefully.

My fists clench. Does this mean Spencer received my gift and wanted to determine who turned Steel's body into Tetris pieces?

"Used to?" I sneer. "Or still does?"

"I don't know," Alaric replies. "I haven't heard from Bram for… a while."

They're keeping something from me. Not that it matters. Anyone associated with Spencer deserves to die.

I arch one eyebrow. "What aren't you telling me?"

"You know all you need to, Ivy," Alaric snaps. "But we need to find Deveraux."

"He's all fucking mine," I hiss. It's a statement, not a question. "I'll bring him in."

"Alive," Alaric says, reading my mind. "I want him alive, Ivy."

I scowl. "Fine, but he's a dead man walking."

CHAPTER 29

BRAM

can't believe I'm back here again. Protecting *him*. Freddie said Spencer was charming when they met, and I don't doubt it. Spencer Bexley only cares about one thing. Himself. Freddie doesn't know about my ties to the monster who hides behind those walls... or what happened five years ago that changed everything.

My hands grip the steering wheel tighter as I gaze up at Bexley's mansion. The streetlights illuminate the cuts on my knuckles from last night's fight. After it happened, I called Freddie, and we returned to the spot. By the time we got there, the man was gone. A bloodstained pavement was the only evidence left behind. I don't know whether to be relieved that I didn't kill him or annoyed we're no closer to finding out more about the Killers Club.

I'm sure it won't be long until we cross paths again.

I sip my now cold coffee and glance at my laptop on the passenger seat. It's seven am. Seb begged me to cover for him this morning. Who knows what happened last night to make him and Callen return so late, but now he owes me two favours.

The curtains twitch on the second floor as Spencer's housekeeper begins her round of cleaning. Soon, his chef will arrive to prepare his breakfast at eight. After that, a personal trainer will follow.

Spencer may seem like your average entitled prick, but he's more than that. He has the brains, connections, and money to kill anyone who looks at him in the wrong way. He wouldn't recognise me if he saw me now. He never paid attention to his drivers. We were disposable, and he treated us like shit on the bottom of his shoes… just like he treated those two girls.

I shiver at the memory. If Freddie discovered Spencer murdered the woman he's been mourning, he'd never have accepted him as a client. Hell, Spencer would need to pay someone else to protect him from Freddie. But I can't tell him. No, I traded my silence for her protection. I'd make the same decision again, even if I'm unsure of whether she survived...

Stop thinking about it, Bram. Push it away.

I get out of the car to patrol the perimeter. I could monitor the extra cameras we installed from my laptop instead, except my legs are cramping, and I need to clear my head.

Steel's death bothers me. How can someone be that good? It should be an open-and-close case. It doesn't take long to solve a murder when I can hack into most computers and CCTV feeds, but still *nada*. I pulled an all-nighter, yet I'm no closer to finding his killer. It was a calculated hit. Too perfect. A power outage in that area at the exact time someone snatched Steel from his bed to be chopped into pieces wasn't a coincidence.

I slope around, re-familiarising myself with the street. Nothing out of the ordinary here. Why couldn't Freddie find someone else to do this? Sometimes he contracts our surveillance work to others, and they work for our shadow security firm, Royal Protection. It saves us from freezing our balls off.

I stifle a yawn and send Seb a text.

Custard creams x5 packets.

That's the first of my many demands for treating me like his bitch. I don't drink anymore, but biscuits are my weakness. Some people think custard creams are at the bottom of the biscuit tier, but they're wrong. Those motherfuckers are moreish.

As I stroll through the shadows, my mind strays to what would happen if someone tried to sneak past me to kill Spencer. The Dukes protect people, no matter who they are or what they've done. However, this is the first time I've been conflicted over a job. It's easy to separate my emotions, but with Spencer... it's personal. Some people aren't worth saving.

CHAPTER 30

IVY

speak through the crackling radio to Penelope. "He's on the move."

"Are you sure it's him?"

"Positive."

I recognised him instantly. It's hard to miss a man when he's the size of a bear. Most women would find Bram Deveraux hot. I mean, he is. Smoking fucking hot. But he's also the same predator who stalked Jonathon from the bar and bashed his skull into the concrete.

"Copy that," she confirms.

Tracking him was easy when I learned about his link to Spencer. As soon as Penelope hacked into Spencer's neighbour's doorbell camera, facial recognition flagged him.

My car has tinted windows, but I still slide down in my seat as he walks on the opposite side of the street. He stops to stretch, making his muscles ripple through his long-sleeved shirt. Who doesn't wear a jacket in February? He's basically showing them off.

"Yes," I encourage him under my breath. "Keep on walking."

The stupid bastard shouldn't have been so engrossed with his laptop while on guard duty. He was probably jacking one out.

"It's done," Penelope confirms.

Lights in the surrounding houses switch off. A temporary power cut won't hurt anyone. The lingering fog lowers visibility further.

Being here again is unsettling. I hoped the next time I returned would be to hunt Spencer, but he'll have to wait. Bram can whet my appetite while I build up for the main course. Regardless of his mysterious history with Alaric, Bram is the reason Jonathon is wheezing through a tube.

"We have eyes on him," a male voice says down the line. "He's getting close."

I can handle Bram on my own, even though Alaric insisted on me bringing backup. I'm lumped with the twins. The three of us trained together, and their egos are through the roof. They're good fighters, and they fucking know it too. They like to call themselves a double threat, but I've affectionately dubbed them Tweedledum and Tweedledee.

"Thanks, Tweedledum," I reply. His voice is an octave higher than his brother's, so I can tell them apart that way. "Don't let him out of your sight."

"Fuck you," he growls back.

They've never liked their nicknames.

My knee twitches. What's taking them so long? From my position, I see a van crawl along to the side entrance of Spencer's mansion that his staff use—God forbid, he lets the peasants in where people can see. It was the escape route I fled from on the night I left him with the help of his housekeeper.

I steady my breathing to keep myself focused, pushing away the memories of my time there. The Bexley mansion was grander than anywhere I'd ever been before. Spencer promised we could live out a fairy tale… until it turned into a horror story.

"What are you waiting for?" I hiss through the static to the Tweedles. "Take him."

It happens in a blur. The back door of the van flies open, leaving no time for Bram to react. Tweedledum launches at him, tackling him to the floor, while Tweedledee leaps from the driver's side and sinks a needle into his neck.

I hum and watch the bottoms of his shoes being dragged into the back of the van. Finally! I turn the key and follow in pursuit.

"Target apprehended," I radio to Penelope. "We're on our way back to HQ."

Poor Bram will get a nasty surprise when he wakes. He's an enigma. Even Penelope couldn't find much information about him. We know he joined the army, toured in Iraq—probably how he met Alaric—then returned to the UK in his late twenties. He's now thirty-three and owns a business—a shady-sounding phone repair company, which is likely a ruse to cover what he's really doing. Spencer always kept his men off any official books.

"Nice job, Tweedles," I tease, knowing it'll get a rise out of them. "Maybe two are better than one in your case."

In all cases, my mind adds in a dirty whisper. Now is not the time to remember how good it felt to be fucked by Seb and Callen. My brain is a horny bitch with zero understanding of time and place. After I've tortured Bram for information about his link to Spencer and any potential association with the Dukes, I'm excited for my next date with Seb.

Bram may not be on my list of the men who were there the night Daisy died, but if he works for Spencer, he won't leave HQ alive. No one does.

CHAPTER 31

BRAM

fight the vomit rising in my throat. Where the fuck am I? My hands and ankles are tied. My shirt is missing, and my shoulder blades dig into a steel bench as I thrash around. The hairs on the back of my neck stand on end, and a burst of chilling laughter bounces off the damp walls. There are no windows, only sterile strip lights on the ceiling, like in a hospital operating theatre.

"Wakey, wakey, sleepyhead." It's a woman's voice. Her playful tone has an underlying ruthless edge. "I've been waiting for you."

The chains binding me jangle as I shake, but fighting them is useless.

How did I get here?

My head aches as I try to remember. The edges of my memories are blurry, but I remember Bexley's mansion. The streets. A van.

Freddie will be pissed when he finds out they've taken me and left our client vulnerable.

The woman circles my bed. Her hair is a lush red,

trailing behind her like a fiery blaze. Whatever they've used to drug me is still in my system, making my eyes struggle to keep up with her motion. She looms over me at the end of the bench like the Grim Reaper.

She grins. A beautiful smile that makes me shiver. "This might make you dizzy."

With a smooth motion, she flips the bench vertically. My binds lock me in place as the soles of my trainers skim the floor, allowing me to face my captor.

Hang on… *Rose?*

Am I imagining it?

I squeeze my eyelids shut, but she's still there when they open. It's her, alright. I recognise her from the bar. Rose, the woman who is fucking my best friend and whose doorstep I dumped flowers on.

"I'm glad you're awake," Rose, or whatever the fuck her real name is, says. "I've been waiting for you."

I get a better look around now. The room is filled with tools designed to torture. Some are hanging on the walls. Others are laid out on a bench. She hovers her hand, moving it over the implements.

She finally selects a branding iron. "That'll do."

She approaches, brandishing the orange tip that glows from the heat in warning.

"What's wrong?" Rose teases, tilting her head to the side to study me. She's enjoying this. How could my check on her have been wrong? She's not a journalist. Someone must have changed her records. Someone with power and resources. "I want to play a game with you."

She moves the burning point close to my skin but doesn't touch me. Not yet. She's building anticipation, toying with me. Sadistic bitch. The scorching heat tingles as she holds it centimetres away. It's not my first time being tortured. I have scars that are a permanent reminder of my time in the army.

I grit my teeth to stop myself from flinching. She wants a reaction. Her body language is comfortable. She's familiar with these surroundings. It's her safe place. Her gaze is devoid of emotion, and I notice the ring around her irises from contact lenses. Is blue her natural eye colour? I bet it's fake, like the rest of her.

While Seb worried about her having a drink with a Killers Club assassin, none of us stopped to consider she might be one of them. Seb's desires blinded him—us—to what was staring us in the face. He's in danger. We all are.

Rose sighs, disappointed I'm not squealing or begging for mercy. She returns to the bench, placing the iron down carefully and picking a photograph instead.

"Do you recognise this man?" She thrusts it at my face. It's the man from the bar. The one whose face I smashed into the ground. She purses her pouty lips. "You should. You're the one who put him in a coma." *At least he's not dead. Yet.* "I want you to tell me why you followed him and what you know."

I say nothing—obviously. I clench my jaw and prepare myself to endure what's coming next. Whatever Rose does can't be worse than the mental torment I inflict on myself daily. Pain is what I deserve for what I did.

She clicks her tongue impatiently and hisses, "If you won't talk, then I'll make you."

I'd like to see her try. She storms back to her tools. When she whirls around again, she hurtles forward. There's no escape as the scorching iron slams into the centre of my chest, setting my skin on fire. My entire body jolts from the searing pain, as if something is trying to claw its way into me

"Are you feeling more chatty now?" she asks as the smell of burning flesh fills my nostrils like cooking bacon. "I'm good at what I do, Bram."

I open my mouth as wide as I can. For a split second, her eyes widen—*sympathy perhaps?*—then her sinister stare returns.

"So you can't talk." She points the weapon at me like a music conductor. "You can write, can't you? I'm sure Spencer wouldn't hire someone who can't write."

My eyebrows lower. Spencer? Does she think I still work for him?

"What's wrong?" she teases. I clench my muscles as she skims the heated point down my neck. Swallowing will hurt when it blisters. "Isn't Spencer a good boss?"

A ringing phone from across the room interrupts her.

"I hope you don't mind if I answer it," she says, then winks. "At least I don't have to bother with a gag."

When she answers, she puts it on loud speaker. I recognise Seb's voice on the other end of the line instantly. Do they know I'm missing yet? Are they searching for me?

"Yeah, we landed fine," Rose lies casually. She's convincing. "The flight was good, no turbulence. How's your day going?" He starts speaking, but Rose cuts him off, "I'm really sorry, but I have to go. My interviewee has just arrived." Her eyes sparkle as they meet mine. "It might take a while. I've heard he's a difficult subject. I'll have to pull the words out of him."

"Call me later, okay?" Seb asks. I detect the excitement and hopefulness in his tone. How will he react when he discovers the girl of his dreams is a psychotic killer? "We still have a date to plan."

She licks her lips, but she's not speaking to Seb when she replies, "I can't wait."

I try to shake my chains, but they're pulled taut. I have to warn him.

"Sorry for the interruption," Rose purrs, returning her attention to me. I breathe a sigh of relief as she puts down the iron. Unfortunately, it's short-lived as she grabs a pair of pliers. "I'm supposed to be in Dublin for a work trip. Nonetheless, this is so much more fun, isn't it?"

She gets closer. So close that her fresh floral perfume engulfs me, and her perky tits press into my chest. It's been a while since I've been close to a woman, and blood rushes to my cock despite my pain. Thankfully, she's too preoccupied to notice, otherwise my tongue won't be the only body part missing.

"Why don't we get you more comfortable, hm?" Her hands go to unfurl my curled fingers, but I'm quicker. I grab her small wrist. With a flick, I could snap it, but she smirks. "I'm not unreasonable, Bram. If you don't let go, I'll saw through your wrists instead of taking a few fingernails."

My semi wilts as I release her. Seconds later, she tears my fingernail off with a vicious swipe. My muscles clench. True to her threat. I let out a muffled moan in agony.

"I want you to write down all you know about Spencer Bexley," she says, sauntering to collect a pen. She slides it into my grasp. "Can you do that for me? A nod will do."

The pen falls from my slippery grip and hits the floor. She sighs in frustration, producing a knife from under her sleeve like a masterful magician. She'd be beautiful if she wasn't holding a blade to my crotch. Full lips, fair skin, a curvy body to die for, and cute freckles covering her nose. Sadly she's the devil in disguise.

"I can be very persuasive."

She twists the knife into my burning wound, making me gasp. Sweat drips down my forehead as the blade travels to the waistband of my jeans, leaving a bloody scratch behind. She presses the sharp point into my dick. "Didn't you hear what happened to the last man who crossed me?" She chuckles affectionately. "Spencer must be busy putting his body back together."

The colour drains from my face. It was her. She killed Anthony Steel. Rose is the killer Spencer is afraid of and who the Dukes are protecting him from. She's more than twisted; she's downright depraved. I was scared before, but now… I'm fucking terrified.

"We can do this the easy way or the hard way." Rose forces the pen back into my hand. "I want to know about Spencer. I want to know how you found Jonathon, and I want to know everything you know about a group who call themselves *the Dukes*."

She's onto us. My mind races as she grabs a clipboard. Maybe it's better if she thinks I work for Spencer. I need to put distance between myself and the Dukes to keep Seb and the others safe.

I drop the pen again, on purpose this time. She punches me square in the face. I don't react, staring back at her in defiance, needing to make my act convincing and letting her think my loyalty lies with Spencer. She hits me again and again. Unencumbered rage pours from her until her chest is heaving from exertion.

"You're going to tell us everything you know about Spencer Bexley," she seethes menacingly, holding a knife to my throat. "Or I'm going to slit your neck open and drain every drop of blood from your body."

Suddenly, the door bursts open. A man I haven't seen for five years walks in.

"Ivy." His voice comes out in a commanding growl. "That's enough."

CHAPTER 32
FREDDIE

"Fuck!" Callen boots the bookshelf, making the spines shake. He loves theatrics. He's mad about Bram being missing and us being outsmarted, but me? I'm fucking furious.

Danny's death forced us to act out of pride, which was purely business. Bram's disappearance is personal. He'd never abandon a car or a job. Someone took him. We won't stop until we find him and, whoever has him, will pay.

"Are you sure there's nothing on the CCTV?" Callen asks for the second time.

"Do you want to check for a third time?" I snarl. "I already told you, there's nothing."

A power cut at the exact moment Bram disappeared has left us with no leads to follow—just like what happened on the night of Steel's abduction. Someone well-trained planned an ambush. Undoubtedly, the same people are behind both cases, but the question is whether the Killers Club or someone else with a grudge against Bexley is responsible. A nagging feeling in my gut tells me this isn't as simple as it appears. We're missing something vital, and we need to figure it out fast.

Callen kicks the wall. While he's intent on damaging all our furniture, Seb is busy talking on the phone. What the hell is he doing? His puppy dog eyes tell me who he's speaking to instantly. As soon as he hangs up, I turn on him.

"Couldn't you wait to check in with your new girl-friend?" I demand. My eyes narrow in fury. He needs to remember where his loyalty lies. Dukes first. Always. "Bram is missing. Do I need to remind you of your priorities?"

"No," he murmurs, averting his gaze and chewing his lip. At least he has the decency to look guilty and isn't making excuses.

What's so special about the new woman in his life? He's obsessed. When we're not focused on getting Bram back, I'll dig into Rose Hathaway's background myself. Seb promised she wouldn't be a problem, but now I'm not so sure.

"Trust me," Callen intervenes with a smile. "Rose has made it wholly clear Seb's not her boyfriend."

Callen grabs a discarded packet of custard creams from the table and tears it open. He crunches loudly, spraying crumbs everywhere.

Seb whirls around, ready to charge at him. "I bought them for Bram."

My nostrils flare. That's enough bickering.

I rarely raise my voice, but I do now.

"Do you think this is funny?" Both of them jump at my words, and I show them Steel's gristly remains on my phone screen. "This could be Bram if you two don't get your heads out of your arses to find him."

Their faces fall. Seb mumbles an apology, and Callen pops the rest of the biscuit into his mouth. Callen won't apologise. He never does. Sorry isn't in his vocabulary.

"Just what we need," I grumble as my phone rings and Spencer's name flashes up. "Both of you shut the fuck up and do something—*anything*—useful while I handle this." I break off from them to answer his call gruffly. "What?"

"I haven't seen the Dukes patrolling this morning," Spencer drawls, dragging out his syllables in a way that makes me want to force the phone he's calling from down his throat. "Is there a problem?"

"There's no problem," I lie. "You hired us because of our discretion. If you don't notice us, that means we're doing our fucking job."

Spencer splutters. "I thought that—"

"That we'd be visible to scare off the bogeyman?" I laugh coldly. "We're not your lapdogs, Bexley. We work our way. If you have a problem with that, we—"

"There's no problem," he interrupts. "What about an up—"

"You'll get an update when I'm ready," I say, ending the conversation.

Seb and Callen stare at me, open-mouthed, in a mixture of awe and shock as I hang up. I pride myself on our fantastic customer service, but Spencer makes my skin crawl. Besides, we've got more pressing issues to contend with than being polite to an entitled prick.

"What?" I bark at them. "Seb, hire security to tail Bexley. Callen, get the car ready. We've got places to be."

We hire security subcontractors to help sometimes. The Dukes can't be everywhere at once, and some jobs don't require our undivided attention. Besides, if the person targeting Spencer has Bram, I need to keep my men where I can see them. We can't lose anyone else. The bastards drive me up the wall, but they're my family. They're all I have, and I'm not losing anyone else. Not again.

I've already lost too much.

CHAPTER 33

IVY

"What?" I spin to see Alaric darkening the doorway like a supervillain. Did he have to charge in and throw his weight around like that? I huff and cross my arms sulkily, like a kid getting a bollocking from a teacher. "You asked me to extract information. That's exactly what I'm doing."

"You're too close to this," he says. "I asked you to find out why he followed Jonathon, but you seem to be more interested in another subject."

Doesn't he understand this beast of a man is the closest I've got to learning more about Spencer? When I captured Steel, I was overpowered by bloodlust and didn't ask him questions. It's been five years since I left the country. A lot could have changed since then. Spencer might operate differently, and I need the details. How else am I going to avenge Daisy?

Alaric's hard features soften, reading my mind. He can keep his pity. He doesn't need to save me anymore. I'm not a pathetic damsel in distress; I can fight my own battles.

"Let me speak to him," Alaric insists.

He words it as a request, even as his voice is firm. It's an order. I look from Bram to Alaric. My head and heart war with each other, but my sensibilities win out.

"Fine, but I'm not leaving," I grumble and step aside, then shoot Bram a sweet smile. "I still have the pliers, if you need them."

"I never thought we'd ever see each other again," Alaric says, casting Bram in his gigantic shadow. "What were you doing sneaking around outside Bexley's mansion?"

Bram winces. Sure, he's in pain from his lovely new branding and exposed nail bed, but there's something hiding under his expression. His mouth curls like Spencer's name makes him sick. I recognise that expression. It's the same one I have whenever I look in the mirror and think about what Spencer's done.

"I've spared your life once before, Deveraux. I won't do it again," Alaric warns. His voice sends goosebumps racing up my arms. Alaric is at a point in his career where he doesn't need to get his hands dirty. He loves violence as much as the next person but gets answers in other ways. "I'll let you live if you give us useful information."

Alaric hands Bram the pen. This time, he doesn't drop it. What's Bram's deal? Doesn't he like a woman telling him what to do? Men are ridiculous. If they weren't so busy dragging their balls along the ground, they might be able to see me coming before I kill them. Their masculinity is a weakness.

"You'll have to forgive Ivy's indiscretions," Alaric says as he paces back and forth. "But I'm sure you, of all people, understand her anger towards Spencer Bexley."

"What do you mean?" I ask sharply. "How can he possibly understand?"

"Because Bram is the one who brought you to me the night Spencer tried to kill you." Alaric's voice is steady. He's telling the truth. This is what he and Stephanie have been hiding from me.

"Him?" I look at the man mounted on the bench like Christ on the crucifix. "He's the one who saved me?"

CHAPTER 34

BRAM

She reaches for the bench, clutching onto it to steady herself. This is a shock. She's never heard about me before.

It's her… *Ivy Penrose.*

The sister of the love of Freddie's life.

I recognise her name from the grave in the cemetery. Two matching headstones next to each other. When I visited to lay flowers with Freddie, I hoped Ivy's coffin was empty and prayed Alaric saved her.

I shouldn't have trusted him. Alaric claimed to run a witness protection programme, but he lied. He has a very different operation. It's genius. What better people to turn into killers than those who are supposed to be dead?

I wanted her to be safe, but I handed her to a man who turned her into a brutal monster. The girl I swore to protect is now a killing machine threatening the people I care about most. Maybe Ivy would have been better off if I left her to die that night. Spencer called me after it happened to drive their getaway car, but I saw what they did and went back for her.

"Why didn't you tell me?" Rose—Ivy—turns on Alaric. Her eyes flicker to my torso and the wounds she's inflicted. Is she capable of feeling guilt? "You should have said something."

"I thought it'd be nice for Bram to see you again." Alaric shrugs. "A nice reunion."

Times like this is when I'd like to speak. If I could, I'd roar. He promised to give her a better life, not train her to take them. He's exploited a vulnerable woman on the brink of death.

"But you—" Ivy argues, as he waves a hand to quieten her. Her face reddens as she resists the urge to retaliate.

Alaric addresses me again, "You've been true to your word and kept your silence for her protection."

I struggle, and he laughs. My silence didn't protect her from Alaric. I'd never have brought her to him if I knew what she'd become; I'd have done everything in my power to save her myself.

"Struggling won't help, Bram," he says. "You should save your energy."

"If he works for Spencer, why isn't he on my list?" Ivy demands.

Her list?

"Patience, Ivy," Alaric says, patting her arm sympathetically. "I want to learn what our guest was doing at Bexley's mansion."

From the smug grin on his face, he already knows. Dread twists in my gut. If he finds out I'm a Duke, the others are as good as dead... if he hasn't found them already.

"I know you stopped working for Spencer Bexley the day you brought Ivy to me," Alaric says. "Then you disappeared off the face of the earth. I thought you had left the country, but can you imagine my surprise when I found out you were back again?"

So what? I narrow my eyes. *Spit it out, motherfucker.*

"You're one of them, aren't you?" Alaric snarls. "The Dukes. The gang getting in our way and killing our clients. We don't take kindly to that."

I shake my head quickly, too quickly. My denial means nothing. He's already made up his mind.

"He's a Duke?" Ivy asks. "How can you be so sure?"

Alaric tuts and takes a phone out of his pocket. "Because of this."

That's mine. Even if my body language doesn't give me away, a message from Freddie—under a code name—about the Bexley job would. Fuck. Thankfully, there's nothing on the device they can use to track the others. We have a strict communication protocol in place. We use a VPN to mask where messages are coming from, and an emergency alert goes out with a location pin if someone doesn't check their phone after a set amount of time.

"We disabled all of your security measures and hacked into your little vigilante group chat," Alaric says. "Impressive tech, by the way. Did you do that yourself?"

Go to hell.

"Your friends don't know where to find you," he mocks. "It's hard to get a signal this far underground."

If Alaric knows I'm a Duke, why am I still alive? I rattle my chains. Ivy should have killed me. At least I'd have died not knowing the truth about the girl I risked everything to protect.

"I know you won't tell us who they are, so I have a better idea," Alaric says. "The Dukes like to play games, and so do we. We'll ask your friends to meet us, and when they do, we'll kill all of them. If they don't show, we'll track them down one by one, then kill you after you've watched them die."

A twisted smile breaks over Ivy's face. "Game on."

Little does she know, she's signing the death warrant of her new boyfriend…

CHAPTER 35

CALLEN

Freddie's shoulders tense as he clutches his phone and shakes in anger. The veins in his arms bulge from his tight grip.

"What is it?" I ask, leaning away quickly to keep my distance in case he hurls it in a fit of rage. At least I'm safer in the backseat.

Freddie rarely loses his temper, but he's like a volcano when he blows, and you don't want to be standing in his way.

"I've got a text," Freddie says through gritted teeth. "From Bram."

Seb looks up from Bram's laptop. We've been trawling it for leads after bringing his abandoned car back to our garage. All we've found is a list of people who want Spencer Bexley dead. Unsurprisingly, most of them have a penchant for violence.

"And?" I prompt. "What does it say?"

"It's a date and location," Freddie says, breathing like a bull about to charge. "The Conservatory. Six pm."

I frown. A poncy restaurant with a dress code. "It wouldn't be my first choice for a ransom negotiation."

"That's because you eat like an animal," Seb rebuffs.

The wee lad's ego is stung after our threesome. I rarely go back to the same girl twice. My cock's fickle. Why fuck the same woman when every hole is a goal? But Rose intrigues me. I'll make an exception for her. There's more of her to explore…

"It's a setup," Freddie states the obvious.

"So, what do we do?" Seb asks. "We can't just leave Bram. We don't know who he's with and what they want. He could be with Steel's killer. It could be an agent from the Killers Club. We don't know what we're walking into."

"We'll be fine," I dismiss his concerns. "Just give me time to raid the cabinet, and I'll have it sorted."

I'm a man of many talents. As well as my ability to do heart surgery, I tinker with gunpowder in my spare time. I'm getting pretty good at it, too.

"No explosives," Freddie and Seb say in unison.

They need to get over the fact I almost set off an inactive landmine in the kitchen. It only happened once.

"Jeez. What are you? The fun police?" I roll my eyes. They need to lighten up and live a little. "We still need ammo."

"It's a public place," Freddie says. "A busy street with lots of people around. They can't have a shoot-out without drawing attention to themselves."

"They haven't given us any proof of life," I say, voicing what they're too afraid to say. "Bram could be riddled with maggots by now."

Seb glares at me in the mirror. Skirting around an issue doesn't change reality. We don't live in a world full of sunshine and rainbows; darkness and death surround us.

"There's a chance he's alive, so we're going," Freddie says. "Bram is a Duke."

His hacking ability is the only reason why he's worth saving.

"We don't know how many of them will be there," Seb says. "We could be outnumbered."

Ten men are the same as one of me. We'll be fine. Sebastian needs to strap on his big-boy boots if he's going to save Bram from the scary kidnappers. It's no surprise Rose wanted to experience a real man.

"Pussy." I cough. "Don't you want to get your hands dirty? You're turning soft since meeting Rose."

A vein twitches on Seb's forehead. "Don't test me, Callen, or it'll be your blood over my hands."

"Enough," Freddie snaps. His brow sets as the cogs in his mind whir, weighing the pros and cons. "We have to be cautious. We'll split up. I can blend in and assess the threat. You two can wait outside."

"Are you trying to suck the joy out of everything?" I groan. "If that mute motherfucker gets us killed, I swear I'll—"

"We have to get ready," Freddie cuts me off coldly. "The Dukes don't leave anyone behind."

CHAPTER 36

IVY

wait in position, perched on a stool and engaging in flirty banter with the bartender. I've been here for two hours, and "Bethany" has just left. If anyone's watching, they'll see I have a reason to be here. No one would question two women innocently catching up over Mojitos.

I text Seb to pass the time.

I'm back in London. How about tomorrow night?

Usually, he's quick to reply, but I get radio silence. Maybe he's playing hard to get.

"Would you like another drink?" the bartender asks, ogling my tits spilling over the top of my dress. "It's on me."

"Maybe later," I say, holding up my half-full glass.

From my spot, I have a perfect view of the doors. I survey the floor. How am I supposed to know who the Dukes are? If their name is anything to go by, I'm half-expecting them to waltz in on horseback in medieval costumes. But I know better than anyone that appearances can be deceiving.

Alaric, the Tweedle twins, and Stephanie are waiting outside with a tied-up Bram in tow. They're parked in a food delivery van. The same van that makes drops to the restaurant every day. Tweedledum even dropped off a few packages to avoid drawing suspicion. We're thorough.

I sip my cocktail patiently. If I got my way, Bram would be dead already. He may have been my saviour once, but that doesn't change the facts. If he worked for Spencer that night, he must have been involved in what happened and belongs on my list. A good deed doesn't cancel out a bad one; saving my life doesn't mean I'll spare his.

The bar buzzes with conversation. It's fancy and upmarket, with jazz music playing in the background. People rest their drinks on nearby tables and stand around chatting, while others gather in groups to share overpriced tiny plates.

My tiny earpiece is hidden behind my hair, and I have my lipstick knife stashed in my bag. Alaric stripped me of all other weapons after my outburst and launched into a lecture about how he doesn't want emotions to cloud my judgement. My judgement isn't clouded. In fact, I see more clearly than ever that I need my cold, brutal revenge.

"We have half an hour to go," Alaric says in my ear. "All clear on the inside?"

The bartender catches my eye and grins. A grin that says he'd like to get into my pants. He'd be so lucky.

"How about that drink?" I ask the bartender. Who am I to turn down a freebie when I've got time to kill? "A Pornstar Martini."

"How is it fair she gets to be on the inside?" Tweedledee grumbles.

I roll my eyes. What a brat. It'll taste all the sweeter knowing he's jealous.

The bartender mixes it up and slides it over. It's garnished with half of a passionfruit, and the seeds have spilled over its frothy surface. "Here you go."

"Perfect," I say, slurping it loudly for the benefit of the Tweedles. "Mmm, delicious."

I glance around again. As I do, someone catches my eye. They're looking right at me. A face I never thought I'd see again.

No. It can't be…

My mind catapults back five years. His thick hair is peppered with more grey, which only adds to his sex appeal. Why now? Why does a sexy silver fox have to stroll back into my life in the middle of a mission?

It's too late to turn away. We're drawn together like magnets. Our gaze meets, and electricity sparks, fizzing across an invisible wire and heightening my senses. I convinced myself that I had imagined this feeling. How could a chance meeting with a stranger have felt so right? Yet seeing him again erases my doubt and proves me wrong. The connection we shared then was real, even if the colour is now draining from his face like he's seen a zombie rise from the dead.

"We have a problem," I murmur, hiding my moving lips behind my hand as the gorgeous man makes his way towards me. "Someone's recognised me."

CHAPTER 37
FREDDIE

s my mind playing tricks? It wouldn't be the first time I'd mistaken someone else for her. Except when her head turns, and the light hits her face to illuminate her features, I'm certain.

Her hair has grown, and it's a deeper shade of red, but it's her. *Daisy.* I'd never forget her face. The face of the woman I've been mourning and whose grave I've visited every month for the past five years.

When I didn't hear from Daisy again, I wanted to find her. I thought she might have lost my number because I couldn't accept that she wouldn't contact me after our meeting. Social media turned up empty. Daisy seemed to have disappeared off the face of the earth. I questioned whether she made up an entire identity until I found an article. A short one, nestled in the pages of a newspaper, about a freak car accident that killed two women on the night we met. I knew it was her instantly.

The Dukes think I'm crazy. How can you know after one night, one drink, one life-changing kiss, that you've met the person you're destined to spend the rest of your life with? I can't describe it. I'm a logical person, and it makes me sound like a madman, yet it's true.

Our chemistry is unlike anything I've ever experienced. It's an ache deep in my bones, like she fills a gap I didn't know was missing. Safety, excitement, an overwhelming urge to do anything to keep her safe, including killing anyone who stands in our way.

She is the one. My one.

I blink, completely thrown off my goal. I'm here to negotiate a ransom because Bram's life is at stake, but I'm frozen to the spot and staring into the face of a ghost.

Callen and Seb are parked a few streets away, awaiting further instruction. Whoever lured us here to talk doesn't want to strike up a friendship. They'll want money or our lives, or, more than likely, both.

She can't be here.

It's too dangerous.

I jump into action. Time slows to a crawl as I wade through the sea of people towards the bar. She lifts a glass to her lips, then halts, as her gaze finds mine. Everything else falls away.

She remembers.

My heart pounds. I shove bodies out of my way like I'm storming through the middle of a battle. Her stare stays fixed on mine. She's equally as stunned. When I finally reach her, we don't speak. We can't. Words aren't enough.

How is this possible? Callen always said I'd lose my sanity pining over a dead girl. Maybe it's finally happened...

I want to stroke her soft skin and feel the blood running through her veins. I have to confirm she's real, but I don't move. My arms stay pressed to my sides, and I tilt my head to examine her. Her skin is glowing, and she's gained weight in all the right places. She's even more beautiful than I remember, but something is different.

"Daisy, your eyes." Even the passing of time wouldn't let me forget those deep brown eyes. They've haunted my dreams for years. "They're blue."

"Freddie… I can… explain."

Her voice is strangled and choked, but all I fixate on is my name rolling off her tongue and how fucking good it sounds. She remembers me. She knows who I am. That has to mean something, doesn't it? I make a snap decision.

"We can't be here," I say. The bartender's jealous gaze burns into me, and I glare at him to back off. "It's not safe."

"Why?" she asks, frowning. "What's wrong?"

"I'll explain everything later," I reply, reaching for her hand. Our fingers brush for a split second. A crackle of energy surges between us, making her wobble atop the high stool. Her eyes widen in bewilderment. "Do you trust me?"

She swallows hard, then nods hesitantly.

My jaw sets in determination. I need to get us out of here. Callen and Seb can deal with the fallout, but Daisy's too important. I've lost her once before, I won't lose her again.

I check my watch. The Killers Club will be here any second. Dragging a woman out of a bar will raise unwanted attention. Against my better judgement, I stay put. We look like an ordinary couple to anyone watching.

"Follow my lead," I say, closing the gap between us. I stroke her cheek, caressing her warmth. Keeping my emotions in check is a struggle. "I thought you were dead."

"I should be," she replies, playing with the hem of her dress and shifting uncomfortably. "It's a long story."

What happened? Where has she been? And why is kissing her all I can think about? Seeing her is like stepping into a dream. Am I dead too? Bram's kidnappers could have killed me. All of this could be a figment of my imagination. My body acts of its own accord. Before I can stop myself, I lean in and my lips graze hers.

She jerks back abruptly, sending an invisible bucket of water sloshing over my head. This isn't a dream.

"I-I'm sorry," I stammer. Am I trying to scare her away? "I shouldn't have."

Years have passed. I'm a stranger. Did I expect her to fall into my arms like I'm Prince Charming? I'm lucky she doesn't slap me. She's not wearing a ring on her finger, but it's plausible she met someone else.

Then she smiles. It lights up her entire face, drawing attention to her cute dimples.

"Kiss me again," she says.

This time, I don't hold back. She wraps her arms around my neck and rises from the stool. Her kiss reminds me of everything I could lose and what I have to fight for. We're in danger; the longer we stay, the more she's at risk.

I step away grudgingly.

"That was…"

Her parted lips make my cock twitch, but our proper reunion can wait a little longer. You'd think waiting ten minutes would be easy after five years, but the prospect is torturous.

"We have to go," I insist. She barely has time to grab

her bag before I take her hand and tug her through the bar after me. "Follow me."

"Where are we going?" she asks, almost tripping over her feet to match my pace. "What's happening? Freddie, you're scaring me."

"Just hold on tight, and whatever happens…" I squeeze her hand. "Don't let go."

CHAPTER 38
CALLEN

Freddie said no explosives. Killjoy. His instructions were clear, but I'm the Duke of Chaos. Rules are there to be broken, and if we're walking into a trap, I'd like to even our odds.

We fly our drone over the building from a few streets away. I don't give a fuck if they see it. They won't know where it's coming from.

"There," Seb says, pointing at a delivery van parked around the back of the building on the tiny screen in his hands. There's limited parking near the Conservatory —*welcome to London*—and all the other cars on the road are empty. "It has to be them, doesn't it? They wouldn't come without a vehicle."

"Not if they know what's good for them," I reply gruffly as I direct the drone back to us, avoiding a near-miss from a plump pigeon. "What do you say? Are you ready to storm the van?"

We haven't heard from Freddie and are waiting for his signal. What's taking him so long? My palms itch with anticipation. I can't sit still, jiggling my feet to shake off the adrenaline pulsing through me. It's the same before every kill. Saving Bram's life is essential, but I'm more excited about a fight. I'm craving it.

The drone returns safe and sound. I get out to retrieve it, taking a deep breath and letting the air fill my blood-thirsty lungs.

"What if something happened inside?" I say, returning and trying to plant doubt in Seb's mind. "Don't you think we've waited long enough?"

Seb checks the time for the fourth time. He's getting nervous. It's not like Freddie to go AWOL. He's the type of crazy bastard who reads flat-pack furniture instructions multiple times before trying to assemble it. I'm usually the one who storms in and breaks the pieces that don't fit together.

"Fine," Seb agrees reluctantly. It's on him to make the call. "Let's go."

I grin and unzip my backpack to check everything is ready. Inside is a small device that I brought in case of an emergency. It's not the only one I have on me, but it's better if Seb thinks so. He's a stickler for following Freddie's precious rules.

"Freddie won't be happy you brought that along," Seb says, putting the cab into gear. "Didn't you hear us saying no explosives?"

This car is one of my personal favourites. Apart from my collection of Harleys, it's the only vehicle I contributed to the Dukes' fleet. A black London cab blends in anywhere in the city, and they're difficult to get hold of.

"This little thing?" I smirk, patting the metal in my bag like a baby's head. Setting it off won't kill anyone, but it'll cause a bang and enough smoke to lure them from a hiding spot. "It's not an explosive, technically…"

Seb swears under his breath as we get caught in a queue at a set of traffic lights. This is why I don't like driving cars. I'm a free spirit, preferring to weave through the traffic on a bike. Cars are too quiet. Where's the roar and wind whipping through your hair? One wrong swerve, and you're dead. That's the kind of risk I live for.

"Pull over," I say as we approach the Conservatory. "I'll find Freddie, and you can park."

"Fine," Seb grumbles. He's gripping the wheel like he's trying to choke it. "But as soon as I hear noise, I'm getting out."

I grab a thermal food delivery bag from the footwell and pull my cap down lower, casting my face in shadow.

"I have everything covered," I say smugly. "I'll see what's going on."

I slam the door behind me and hum as I head to the alleyway where we saw the van. Yeah, I lied to Seb. So what? I can find Freddie later. They'll all be thanking me when I save their arses.

I talk loudly into my phone about picking up a fake food delivery order.

"Fuck!"

I trip over my feet and land on my knees. The stinging pain makes me grin, but I don't get up straight away.

A device tumbles out of my bag during the fall. Oops. My handmade creation rolls toward the van like a tennis ball. A phrase my dad used to say comes back to me. *Ask for forgiveness, not permission.* It didn't apply when he beat my mam, but it sure as hell applies here.

I stand to brush myself down, watching it sneak underneath the vehicle.

One...
Two...
Three.

CHAPTER 39
FREDDIE

"Why are we leaving this way?" she asks, mumbling an embarrassed apology to the staff as we cut through their kitchen. "You know there's a front door, don't you?"

"Trust me," I say, ignoring the staff's confused glances. "This is—"

A loud noise outside makes everyone jump. *Callen.* What happened to not bringing explosives? Just when I think he doesn't need a babysitter anymore, he pulls shit like this.

"It's probably a car exhaust," I lie dismissively.

The staff doesn't look convinced, but they nod and return to chopping vegetables while we continue through a narrow corridor.

"That wasn't a car," Daisy hisses in my ear. "What the hell is going on?"

"Daisy." We turn a corner and stop at the fire exit. I turn to face her. She's involved now. I've pulled her into this. If they saw her with me, she'd be a target. "Whatever happens, stay close to me. I won't let anything happen to you."

She gulps as I throw open the door. Thankfully, Callen has shown some restraint. There's no fire, but the air is thick with smoke, and he emerges through the fog.

"Get behind me," I order Daisy, using my body to shield her.

The van door opens, and three people jump out. They're fast, but I'm quicker. I draw guns from my waistband and point them at the identical twins, while Callen levels his weapon between the eyes of a blonde.

"Where is he?" I demand.

A fourth man steps forward, unfazed by our weapons. He's bald, as tall as me, and covered head to toe in tattoos. He's the leader.

"We meet at last," he says in an unusually deep tone. "You must be the Dukes."

"And you are?"

"You already know who we are," he replies. "Considering you've taken it upon yourself to interfere in our business."

The Killers Club.

This is payback for Adam. We killed him to prove to the Killers Club we were serious, but it was strictly business. Taking Bram is personal. A line has been crossed, and there's no going back.

"Where's Bram?" I demand.

"All you have to do is answer a few questions to get your friend back," he says in a way that implies he'd cut Bram's throat, then hand him over.

"How do we know he's not dead?" Callen pipes up. The woman scowls at him, and he purrs, "You're pretty, sweetheart. But I'd like you better with a hole in your head."

The leader's tattooed face contorts in a furious rage. She's his weak spot. I make a mental note. You never know when you might need to exploit a weakness later.

"Is that the best line you have?" The blonde looks Callen up and down, then laughs. "You know what they say about men with big dick energy?" She holds her pinkie finger up and wiggles it. "They're lying."

If we weren't in a showdown with the best killers in the country, I'd laugh. There's nothing wrong with Callen's ego being knocked down a peg or two.

Callen's cheeks redden. "Bitch."

"That's what they all say, honey," she replies with a wink, then nods to her boyfriend. "If they want proof, let's show them."

The leader grunts, but nods at the twins. They disappear into the shadowy depths of the van and return, holding a limp figure between them. Bram struggles to stand. His chest heaves as he gasps for air. He's covered in bruises, and his clothes are bloodstained.

I try not to react and ask, "What do you want?"

"I want you to stop playing games," the leader says. "We've been in London longer than your little gang, and we're going nowhere. I'm giving you one final chance. You can disband the Dukes and leave the city, or you can die. We're very good at what we do."

"We're not afraid," I answer, narrowing my eyes. He doesn't intimidate me. "You may be good at what you do, but we're just as good."

Our stares lock on each other. Both of us refuse to back down until a rush of air passes me. *Daisy*. She tries to run in her ridiculous heels but isn't quick enough. A twin blocks her, grabbing her by the hair and hauling her back. Her screech makes me shiver. His arm tightens around her neck as he holds her in a headlock.

"Where do you think you're going?" the twin demands, dragging her to stand next to Bram. "You're staying here."

Her eyes reflect fear. My guard slips, and the leader sees it. Just like I saw his drop when he defended the blonde. He knows I care.

The leader cracks his knuckles. "It's time to negotiate."

CHAPTER 40

IVY

I knew this mission was heading south as soon as I saw him. Freddie, the man who made my heart skip a beat five years ago. A fleeting encounter with this handsome stranger preceded the worst night of my life. With the pain that followed, I thought I imagined how good it felt to be with him, but our sizzling connection is still there.

My thoughts are a mess. They come crashing in like a tsunami. Wave after wave of confusion. I put the pieces together as soon as I saw Callen. I should have stabbed that fucker when I had the chance, but Freddie… isn't supposed to be the man we're looking for. If he and Callen are Dukes, is Seb one of them too?

Tension mounts between Alaric and Freddie. I catch Stephanie's eye and hope she can tell what I'm thinking. We can work the situation to our advantage. We want information; I can get it. She inclines her head in a nod so imperceptible that no one else notices.

We're on.

I fake an escape by trying to run. Tweedledum is on me

in a flash. He wraps his muscled arm around my neck, holding on a little too tight. Jeez! He could try to pretend he's not enjoying this. When we're next in HQ, I'll wipe the floor with him in a fight.

Freddie's emotionless exterior crumbles for a fraction of a second, but we all see it. Fear. We're trained to sense it like sharks. What's he afraid of? Does he really care about losing someone he's only met once before?

I whimper like any normal girl would in this situation. Stepping into a role is second nature, but I can't stop thinking about the Dukes' link to Spencer. Bram's refused to write anything down, so all we've managed to infer from a text message is that they have some kind of working relationship. My intuition tells me Freddie is a good guy, but I've been wrong before. Am I wrong again? I need to work out what their connection is.

"Bring her to me," Alaric says.

Tweedledum throws me to the ground at Alaric's feet.

Callen sees me properly for the first time. His eyes widen, more in bemusement than surprise. A grin plays on his lips. Meanwhile, Stephanie makes her move. She charges at Callen, playing into his hands. He responds as expected, pulling her close and holding a gun to her head. He's annoyed about her earlier comment, even though I know his gigantic cock matches his ego.

Alaric growls and forces me to stand by my hair. His grip is gentle, but I feign a painful gasp for dramatic effect. We're manipulating the situation, even though he doesn't like putting his girl in danger. Callen is a loose cannon.

"Don't hurt her," Freddie pleads as Alaric holds a knife to my throat.

He's clueless about me being one of them, but not all the Dukes are ignorant. My gaze strays to Bram, who thrashes against the twin's grip. Tweedledee sinks another sedative-filled injection into his neck before he tries anything or blows my cover.

Alaric swipes the blade over my skin and draws blood. "I could slit her throat."

"And I could paint the street with her brains," Callen responds, pressing the barrel into Stephanie's temple.

He's toying with her. *Twisted bastard.* Making people suffer isn't a job for him. He enjoys it.

"Enough, Callen," Freddie orders, turning to Alaric. "Let's make a deal."

"How about a trade?" Alaric proposes. "One for one. You can't pick both. Then, we can talk real business. Who will you choose?"

He's testing him. Either way, it's a win for us. Freddie's eyes dart between me and Bram. This should be a simple decision. He should pick a Duke over a stranger, yet he says nothing.

A piercing fire alarm coming from the restaurant cuts through our negotiations. Stephanie uses the distraction to twist out of Callen's hold with the elegance of a ballet dancer, while the twins drag Bram's limp body back into the van.

Alaric tucks away his knife and whispers in my ear, "You know what to do, Ivy. Find out everything you can, then kill them all."

"Give me a week," I say, barely moving my lips.

"You have three days," Alaric counters.

I know that if I don't contact him by then, he'll extract me himself.

A gun fires.

A bullet soars past.

Then a roar of agony and pain tears through the air. A

commotion breaks out, and Tweedledum clutches his chest. Blood soaks through his shirt as he topples over, but he's not the one screaming. It's his brother. His scream shakes me to the core. I recognise it—the haunting sound of someone losing the person they love the most, just like how I lost Daisy.

Kitchen staff rush out of the back exit, stumbling onto the scene. The lingering smoke obscures the details, but we must act fast to avoid being seen. I remove my earpiece and crush it underfoot. If the Dukes are sophisticated enough to kill Adam, I can't risk them finding it.

Alaric hurries to Tweedledum, and I start running.

"This way." Freddie's firm hand takes my arm and brings me thudding back to reality. "Daisy, come on!"

Freddie hauls me down the street to catch up with Callen, who is already fleeing.

I peer back over my shoulder to see Alaric through the blur of figures. He slams the van door shut behind them as Stephanie hits the accelerator. The van squeals as she floors it. Innocent bystanders throw themselves out of the way as they hurtle away.

"Look out!" Freddie pulls me to the side to avoid getting mowed down as the van whooshes past. "Hurry up!"

We reach the main street, and a black cab comes to a halt at our feet. The window rolls down. My stomach flips and drops as my earlier suspicions are confirmed.

Seb.

He's a Duke.

"Get in." Freddie pushes me into the backseat and follows in after me as Callen jumps into the passenger seat. "Drive!"

I'm in a car with three men who are now the Killers

Club's number-one enemy. Alaric wants me to kill them all.

"Go after them," Callen roars. "That way!"

Seb turns the wheel in the opposite direction.

"What're you doing?" Callen yells, slamming his hands on the dashboard in frustration. "You're going the wrong way."

Seb ignores him, and his eyes meet mine in the mirror. "Rose? What're you doing here?"

"Rose?" Freddie frowns. "This is Daisy."

"I think I'd know my girlfriend's name, boss," Seb growls. "Daisy's dead, remember?"

Callen smirks, thriving in disarray. "Looks like someone has been telling porkies…"

I've planned for this. All agents must get their cover story straight before entering the field.

"First, I'm not your girlfriend," I correct Seb. "Second, Freddie's right. My real name *is* Daisy Penrose, and… I'm in witness protection."

AUTHORS NOTE

I've had so much fun writing this book, and I hope you've enjoyed reading the start of their crazy journey.

This series would never have been finished, if it wasn't for my amazing husband's support. He's my live-in chef, carrier of heavy book parcels, and the person who keeps reminding me that I *can* do this.

Likewise, I can't thank Ria and Kyla (my talented beta readers) enough for their continued support.

Finally, thank you, the reader, for taking a chance on me. Out of all the books in the world, I feel honoured that you picked up mine.

ABOUT THE AUTHOR

Holly Bloom has a degree in English Literature, but don't let that fool you... she would pick a steamy romance over a Shakespeare play any day!

Holly writes contemporary romance - the dark, gritty and twisty kind. She loves creating badass babe characters, who aren't afraid to speak their minds, and writing about the men who can handle them - often, there is more than one! Why choose, right?

When she isn't working on her next project, Holly spends an unhealthy amount of time watching true crime and roaming around the woods near her home in the UK.

As well as gooey chocolate brownies, Holly's favourite thing in the world is hearing from her readers - her characters may bite, but she doesn't! Promise!

Find out more and sign up to Holly Bloom's newsletter to receive a free book at:
www.hollybloomauthor.com